SHOWDOWN

Grabbing Ben Bolling's collar, Tip shoved him out into the yard, raised his gun, shot out the light, and dodged out, just as a wild yell broke from Jeff.

"Take the kitchen door!"

Tip swung, rammed his gun into Bolling's back, and said, "Make for the wagon shed—and run!"

Bolling ran. Shots poured out of the cook-shack door. A man yelled "There they go!" and fired. Tip spun Bolling around and shoved him against the wall, ramming his gun into his midriff. "You make a move and I'll let this off."

"You wild damn fool!" Bolling whispered savagely. "You won't get away with it."

BOUNTY GUNS

Luke Short

A DELL BOOK

Published by
DELL PUBLISHING CO., INC.
1 Dag Hammarskjold Plaza
New York, New York 10017

ISBN: 0-440-10758-X

Reprinted by arrangement with the author
Printed in the United States of America
Previous Dell Edition #D350 and 0758
New Dell Edition
First printing—August 1976
New Dell printing—November 1979

CHAPTER
1

It could just as well have been any other town but Forks, and any other afternoon but Saturday, but that was the way it happened. Tip Woodring's trail-gaunted chestnut threw a shoe six miles from Forks at high noon on a Saturday, and by the time Forks was in sight he was fast going lame.

Now, Forks, like any town in the cow country, is busy on a Saturday afternoon, and when Tip Woodring rode up to the lone blacksmith shop, he found two teams before him waiting to be shod. He dismounted stiffly, a tall young man, redheaded, with a faintly freckled face that was shaped like a blunt wedge, tough-looking under a week of wiry beard stubble. On the day when the cow country cleaned up, Tip Woodring was wearing a mud-splotched coat, soiled Levi's, and a faded-blue cotton shirt, and it might have been this that the blacksmith objected to when Tip put his proposition.

"All right, you're busy," Tip said. "Let me shoe him myself and I'll pay you what you ask."

"No," the blacksmith said. "Get in line or get out."

That was the first irritation. The second one came minutes later when Tip swung into the barbershop, only to find a dozen men waiting a turn in the chair. He left, hunting another shop, and pushed through the sidewalk crowd to Forks's four corners, where the third one met him face to face. He was crossing the street when a drunk puncher rammed a horse into him, slamming him against the endgate of a spring wagon.

Tip straightened up, his temper edging him, and saw that too many people were between him and the vanishing puncher. A week of hard riding, of cold pan bread and jerky, of mountain rains and desert suns are apt to wire-edge a man's nerves, and when Tip Woodring hit the side-walk, saw the inviting swing doors of the Paradise Keno Parlor before him, and shouldered through them, his gray eyes looked wicked.

He stepped into a big high-ceilinged barroom with a balcony running along all four sides, and roughly shoul-dered his way through the crowd toward the bar to the right. Bellied up to it, he demanded a whisky, then tipped his hat back off his forehead and scrubbed his face with the palm of a callused hand. It was at once a gesture of weariness and an effort to rub out an ugliness of mind.

The percentage girl who came up to him couldn't un-derstand that, however. She made the mistake of putting a hand on his arm and saying, "Buy me a drink."

Tip straightened up and looked down at her. "Go away," he said quietly.

The girl looked over her shoulder, and then, just as the bartender set down the bottle and glass in front of Tip, she poured herself a drink, raised the glass, and smiled coyly at Tip.

The drink never reached her mouth. It was batted from her hand, splattering all over Tip's coat front, and he looked up to see a big man in a fancy vest next to the girl, who had wheeled to face him. The man was half drunk, and his loose-jowled face was ugly as he looked from the percentage girl to Tip.

"Pickin' up the saddlebums again, eh?" he asked the girl.

Tip straightened up and gently shoved the girl to one side. "Just a minute," he said mildly. He poured out a glass of whisky, then carefully threw it all over the punch-er's fancy vest. Setting the glass down, he said pleasantly, "Now go on."

The puncher backed up a step, stared down at his vest, then looked up at Tip and started to curse him.

Tip's voice cut in, and the puncher stopped talking.

"Are your boots screwed to that floor?" Tip asked, his

voice deceptively mild. "Because if they ain't, they're goin' to point to the ceiling in just about a minute."

The crowd immediately around them fell silent, and the puncher stared unbelievingly at Tip, then laughed. He didn't speak. He reached up, pulled his vest aside, and on the pocket of his shirt reposed the badge of the town marshal's office. He let Tip have a good look at it.

"Say that again, and louder," he said.

Tip took a step toward him, spread his legs, and put his hands on his hips. There was a wild look in his eyes now, the look of a man who has been pushed too far and having been pushed, will not retreat. His voice was thick and urgent when he spoke.

"I said you better leave or I'll twist your head off and run away with it and hide it."

What happened then was sudden as thought. The marshal, braced in his tracks, swung viciously at Tip's face. With his left elbow Tip blocked the blow, and with his right he drove a fist into the marshal's face. To a bystander, it seemed as if the marshal exploded off the floor, went off balance, and fell on his back. Before he hit the floor, a man dived at Tip, knocking him against the bar. Tip grabbed the bottle off the bar top, swung it, caught the man in the head, and sent him reeling to trip over the marshal and sprawl on his face.

Tip eyed the circle of watchers and said, "Anybody else feels froggy, now's the time to hop on."

And then, from the balcony, an iron voice said above the murmur of the crowd, "Nobody's going to hop on anything."

Tip didn't glance up immediately, but when the crowd started to back away, he swiveled his head and looked above him. A man dressed in a black townsman's suit was leaning on the balcony rail, a shotgun resting in the slack of his arm. He said, "Joe, hold your greener on them till I get down there."

The bartender pulled out a sawed-off shotgun from under the bar, laid it on the bar top, and regarded the crowd. The man in black walked along the balcony to the stairs, came down them, and by the time he had shoved through the crowd the marshal and the other man were on their feet.

The man in black broke through the circle of watchers and came over to the marshal. His thick, wavy hair, plentifully shot with gray, sat high off a broad forehead that tapered down to a long, pale face which wore a look of ingrained dissipation and alertness. He glanced briefly at Tip, his look friendly, but when he turned to the marshal that friendliness had disappeared.

"Don't bother lying, Cove. I saw the whole thing from the balcony. Take that girl you like so well and get out of here, both of you. And don't come back here asking me to give her work again. She's through."

The marshal glared wickedly at Tip. "He's under arrest," he muttered thickly.

The man in black said mildly, "Better not try it, Cove. You won't make it stick." He stared at the marshal a long time, and finally the marshal turned away. The man in black raised both hands and called, "Drinks on the house, boys. Line up."

He walked over to Tip, who was lounging on the bar, and said, "Come into my office, will you?"

Tip followed him through the door at the rear end of the bar which led into a medium-sized room that was an office. It was lighted by an overhead kerosene lamp against the approaching dusk.

The gambler shut the door behind them, and then put out his hand. "My name's Holman, Rig Holman," he volunteered. He laughed then, as Tip shook hands with him. "I don't know yours, but it's likely Billy Hell."

Tip found himself laughing, too. He told Holman his name, and Holman waved him to a deep leather chair, then walked over to the desk, opened a box of cigars, and offered one to Tip, who refused in favor of his pipe.

They appraised each other frankly for a moment, and then Holman said, "Stranger, aren't you?"

Tip nodded. "Just ridin' through."

"I thought so." He paused. "That was a hell of a risky thing to do, you know."

Tip grinned. "I was mad, I reckon."

Holman dismissed this with a nod. "Ridin' the grub line?" he asked pleasantly.

Tip only shook his head, and Holman looked keenly at him. Then the gambler walked over to the desk and sat on the edge of it, facing Tip.

"I don't know how to go about this, Woodring," he said quietly. "You'll think I'm snooping in your business if I ask questions. I'm not, really. I—I'm just wondering if you're footloose."

"I'm on my way to the short-grass country up in Wyoming," Tip said slowly. "I'm sick of fightin' a dry country."

"Ranching?"

"That's it. I'm goin' to look around."

"And buy a ranch, eh?"

Tip smiled wryly. "When I earn the money."

Holman said quickly, "All right. How would you like to earn it workin' for me?"

Tip didn't answer immediately. He lighted his pipe again, then said, "Quick and dirty-like?"

"Judge for yourself," Holman said. "Want to hear it?"

"If it won't make me deaf."

"Ever hear of Blackie Mayfell, the lucky prospector?" Holman asked.

Tip nodded. "Who hasn't? Sure. He was murdered over on the other side of the Vermilions some time ago, wasn't he?"

Holman nodded, slid off the desk, went around it, and opened a drawer. The paper he took out he handed to Tip. "Blackie came into my office last spring and slapped down fifteen thousand dollars in gold right where I'm sitting. He wanted his life insured."

Tip scowled but said nothing.

"He said he was on to something big, a big body of ore,

but he wanted to prospect it another two months. He was afraid for his life." Holman paused, and still Tip didn't say anything. "Here was his proposition; you can read it in that paper. He'd give me fifteen thousand dollars. If he was alive at the end of two years the money was mine. If he was killed, I was to pay his daughter, Lynn Mayfell, fifty thousand dollars."

There was a moment of silence and then Tip asked, "You took him up?"

Holman nodded, adding, "And paid off the fifty thousand dollars to his daughter after his death."

Tip was still scowling. "Fair enough. What's the kick?"

"I'm not a welsher, Woodring. My payoff proves that." He leaned forward, putting his hands on the desk. "But I don't take a loss like that lying down; I want to find Blackie's killer."

"Isn't the U. S. Marshal's office working on that?"

"Not the way I'm going to work on it," Rig Holman drawled. "I don't give a damn if the marshal's office finds Mayfell's killer—so long as I find him first. I don't even give a damn what they do to him—after I find him."

"I don't get it," Tip said, after a puzzled pause.

"I want my investment back," Holman said quietly. "I'll let somebody else settle the justice end of it."

"Investment back from who?"

"Blackie's killer."

"How do you know he can pay it?"

"Because whoever killed Blackie Mayfell killed him for one thing—the gold Blackie turned up. The killer has got that gold now, and I'll take my thirty-five thousand of it."

Tip's eyes narrowed a little. "Maybe he isn't the kind who'd hand it over to you."

Holman's smile was quick, shrewd. "You think a minute and you'll see why he'll hand it over to me."

It didn't take Tip that long. He said, "I get it. He'll either turn it over to you or you'll turn him over to the law."

"You will," Holman corrected. "That is, if you take the

proposition. There's ten thousand in it for you, if you turn up the killer and bring back thirty-five thousand to me. There's the deal—face up. Is it quick and dirty?"

Tip said softly, "But why pick on me? You never saw me before in your life. How do you know I wouldn't light a shuck once I had your money?"

Holman only laughed and said, "When you hear the rest of it, you may understand. Do you know where Blackie was killed?"

"Not the spot."

"Ten miles from the town of Hagen." He paused. "That town is right in the dead center of that old Shields-Bolling feud."

Tip whistled in low exclamation, and Holman went on. "That war has killed a U. S. Marshal who tried to stop it, four of the Shieldses, and three of the Bollings. And Blackie Mayfell, maybe."

"I've heard of that feud. You think they got him?"

"I don't think. I'm just telling you." Holman nodded toward the barroom. "A few minutes ago you walked into my bar, in a strange town. You didn't know the name of a man in this town. Still, you had brains enough to size up the marshal and comb him over. You were quick enough to see what he would do, and do it before he could. You were quick enough to handle his deputy in the same way. You were tough enough to choose that whole gang. And you were honest enough to pay for two drinks—neither of which you drank—before you came in here." He paused. "I'm a gambler, Woodring. I go by little things. You suit me."

Tip, scowling, rose and walked to the window. The lamps of Forks were lighted against the dusk, and still he did not see them. He was thinking of only one thing. That ten thousand dollars would buy him a spread up in the short-grass country where a man didn't have to drink out of cow tracks, where he didn't have to save for seven years to buy a small herd of beef that could be wiped out in one drouth. He thought of that day when he'd left the south country. Seven years of hard work could be seen from the doorway of his shack—seen and smelled, for the cattle were dead, their bellies bloated, their legs in the air, scattered from the draw to the windmill, which was only pumping air. He had shot the last of them, thrown the key away, ridden to town, collected hide money, and set out for the short-grass country on a gaunted horse. Seven years of it.

He studied the reflection of Rig Holman in the window, watching him. The man had been honest, had warned him of the Shields-Bolling country he would ride into. Tip saw him open a drawer of the desk and lay something on top of the desk. Tip turned, curious.

Holman was watching him. He pointed to a canvas sack and said, "There's three thousand of it right there, if it will help you make up your mind. It's yours now, and will be, luck or no luck. What about it?"

Tip looked at the money and then at Holman and then down at his cracked boots, and he thought, *Why not?*

He discovered that he had not only thought it, but that he said it aloud, and decided immediately that he had made up his mind.

"You're a gambler, too, I see," was all Rig Holman said.

CHAPTER
2

FORKS WAS THE ONLY TOWN on the Big River bench, and the Vermilions, shouldering out of the distant west, were too high, too remote, too impassable to figure in its life. A wagon road started west from Forks, but as it divided at each ranch it became dimmer until, pressed against the steep shoulders of the Vermilion range, it existed only long enough to accommodate the mill in the big timber. Beyond and above that, it shrank into a trail, where a few small scattered bands of cattle made their way to and from the mountain pastures. Above that, it was nothing, and Tip Woodring, pressing into the boulder fields of the peaks in a drizzling early-morning rain, had only his instinct and a few game trails to follow. Hunkered down in his slicker, the rain channeling off his Stetson, he reflected that this was an appropriate introduction to the country. Noon found him twisting through the boulder-shot canyons of the high peaks, leading his horse sometimes, other times feeling his slow way forward and watching for the fall of ground which would announce that he was on the other side.

It came later, and with it a driving rain. Once through the boulder field and into the sparse growth just below timber line, he took the first trail that offered a way to the shelter of the big timber below. Somehow, this west slope of the mountains was different, more forbidding. It was as if the bitter quarrel between the Shieldses and the Bollings, whose country this was, had laid its stern mantle over this slope.

Tip recalled what he had heard of this feud, remembering that the men who came out of this country did not like to talk about it. Years ago, the Shieldses and Bollings, coming onto the tight mountain meadows of the Vermilions' west slope, had settled there, sharing what land they needed equably. Soon their large families attracted a store and other settlers and the beginnings of Hagen town. The cause of the fight was lost in the bitter past; a slurring word at a dance by one of the Bollings when a Shields sweetheart was showing too much favor to a townsman. A fight that night resulted in the death of one of the Bolling boys. It was avenged within the week, this time on the Shields girl's father. Soon, since these families were Texans out of Mississippi, the cousins and uncles and other kin drifted in, making the fight their own. No sheriff could speak his mind safely, no jury could convict, no marshal could get any help. It was a country of suspicion, of unfriendliness, of shots in the dark, of secret funerals, of corrosive hatred, and of sudden death.

At dusk, the trail between the dripping pines dipped sharply, the trees broke away, and below him Tip could see the dark gash of a valley. Down it, where it widened enough, lay a town, its few scattered lights winking in the rain of settling dark.

Tip put his horse onto the valley road, feeling a curiosity edged with sudden wariness. Only a handful of the dark bulking buildings were lighted. At the four corners, he made out the dim lamplit lobby of a shabby hotel and, beyond it, the lighted emptiness of a saloon whose windows were painted white halfway up. He looked across the street then, and in the shadow of a dark doorway he saw two figures flat against the door. They were watching the saloon, and again, riding abreast and past it, Tip settled his attention there. On either side of the door, two men were waiting. A third, at the very edge of the window, was standing on tiptoe, peering into the saloon. Quizzically, Tip's glance traveled to the lamplit interior. Being on horseback, he could see over the white stripe.

Save for one man, elbows on the bar, facing the door that was the entrance from the hotel lobby, the saloon was deserted. Even the bartender was gone. The whitewashed, flyspecked walls, hung with faded calendars, the two empty tables against the back wall, the greasy mirror behind the bar, all stood out in sudden relief. The man lounging there seemed unaware of any interest in him.

At the sound of Tip's horse, the man at the window turned his head, glanced briefly and futilely at the horseman, and then faded back into the dark against the wall. He heard this man say to one by the door, "You better try the lobby again." It was a low voice, drawling, but with an iron undertone of command.

Tip felt a kind of cold and distant wrath inside him, but it did not speak in a voice as loud as caution. It was none of his business, whatever this crew wanted. He went on past a store, also lighted enough for a man to read its sign: *Sig's Neutral Elite.* That brought a faint smile from Tip. Beyond that store was a high board fence, and then the feed barn, proclaimed by its black and yawning arch.

Tip rode into the dark archway and dismounted, and found that he was in the midst of a group of men. They parted for him, silent, and he made his way past four saddled horses toward a lantern on the floor. By its light, a man was saddling a fifth horse. He looked briefly, unenthusiastically, at Tip and said, "Take any stall."

Tip unsaddled, running his hand over his weary chestnut, pressing the water off his hide in dripping rivulets. He rubbed him dry with a towsack, listening. The hostler, leaving the lantern where it was, went forward leading the horse. He came back just as Tip unstrapped his thin war bag from the cantle, and did not look at Tip.

Tip listened, waiting for voices that did not come, then picked up his war bag and said to the hostler, saddling a sixth horse, "Grain him."

"All right."

Tip tramped down the centerway, swerving for the restless horses. Again these men, watching the street, parted for him without a word, closing their ranks behind him as he stepped out onto the boardwalk dappled with rain. Something was about to happen here, he reflected.

Far down the street a light went out, and that was all.

The man at the corner of the saloon's window did not speak as Tip passed. He seemed to be looking upstreet. At the saloon door, there was only one man now. Tip hesitated, came to a sudden decision, and put a hand on the doorknob. The man spoke immediately and courteously. "I wouldn't go in there."

Tip shoved the door open six inches. The light from the saloon lamp suddenly blossomed through the crack, and Tip saw the face of the man who spoke to him. It was a young face, wild and strained, the face of a boy in his teens.

Tip said quietly, "I want a drink, that's all," waited a moment for the kid to answer, then stepped inside and closed the door behind him.

He understood it now, looking at the man at the bar. This man was drunk, very drunk, and he held a six-gun in his hand. He was dressed in wet range clothes that had pooled the floor with dark spots. He was stocky, young, and square and tough-looking, with a sagging, good-humored face whose dark eyes were struggling to focus. The gun in his hand came up, halted, and was steady enough.

Tip said again, quietly, "I want a drink, that's all." He waited a moment, and when the man didn't speak, Tip walked on. He went behind the bar, removed his slicker, took down a bottle of whisky, and filled a glass, all under the undecided gaze of the stranger.

Then, from the lobby door, came the iron voice he had heard before. "Buck, come here."

The puncher whirled, pointing his gun at the oblong of dim light, and saw nothing. He laughed softly, drunkenly, to himself.

A new sound came to Tip then, the sound that in these last months he had learned to hate. It was the sound of many horses running.

The man in the lobby yelled, "Get down, Buck!"

The window glass crashed, slivering at its outer edge. A gun barrel poked through, aimed at the ceiling, and exploded. The overhead lamp whipped out. For one brief second, Tip held the whisky glass in his hand, watching the lobby door. The light there went out, too, but Buck's unmoving figure was still framed in it. Tip whipped up his gun and in a wide, clouting arc, he aimed the barrel of it at Buck. He felt it hit, heard Buck slump to the floor, and then he melted behind the bar. A man shouted then, out on the street, and the blast of a shotgun sent a section of the saloon window jangling to the floor. Three shots hammered out from across the street, on top of the second blast from the shotgun. Its load boomed into the bar, rocking it. A wild fire of shots started to pour in from the street. By the orange gun flashes, Tip could see a mad tangle of horses out there in the mud. He heard a man yell wildly, and then the pounding of feet from the lobby. Suddenly, in the far corner of the barroom, from beside the gaping window, two guns opened up toward the street. A horse screamed, and then the whole tangle outside seemed to dissolve in the sound of running horses.

Tip lay there on the floor behind the bar, letting the silence settle around him again.

He heard a man say softly, "Buck," and when Buck did not answer, the man stepped through the broken window. Somebody sloshed through the mud, hit the boardwalk running, and said, "Did they get him?"

"Go through the lobby and get that rider. Where's Pate?"

"Here," the kid answered.

"Come in here with me. Be sure before you shoot."

Tip rose slowly, backing out from behind the bar, putting his back to the wall.

"Buck," someone called again. Tip could see him, framed in the broken window.

"He's all right," Tip said quietly.

The man shot then at the direction of his voice.

Anger flicked up and died, and Tip moved stealthily along the wall, feeling his way. Suddenly he put his hand on somebody's slicker sleeve, and the arm yanked away violently.

In a kind of blind panic Tip swung then, and he felt his fist settle in the hollow of a throat. He heard the throttled cry, the crash of a table tipping over, a body hit the floor.

A voice said from the middle of the room, "Have you got him, Cam?"

Tip said wickedly, "Damn you, I'm holding a gun on you and I can see you! I want out of here! Buck's all right!"

There was a long pause, then the same iron voice said, "Strike a light, then."

"Strike it yourself!" Tip said savagely. "I'll hold my gun."

There was indecision in the man's immobility. He said, "If you're a Bolling kin, you're a dead man."

"If I was, Buck would be dead now," Tip said, his voice still sharp in anger.

There was another long moment of waiting, and then Tip saw the man make a move. Suddenly a match flared, and the shadows took form. The man regarding him might have been an older, harder, more disillusioned, more humorless replica of the Buck who lay at his feet. He had a craggy, bitter face that could have been chiseled out of leather-colored stone. Only his eyes, hot and wicked and ruthless, and a raw and livid scar running from temple to jaw on his right cheek seemed alive. The scar at the temple throbbed steadily.

"Put that gun down," he said. His was the iron voice that Tip had heard before.

"Not till I'm ready," Tip said softly.

There was a long silence, during which Tip wondered if the man would shoot when the match died. But he didn't. He said to the boy next the bar, "Light that lamp, Pate."

Pate struck a match and pulled down the lamp. When its glow mounted, Tip saw the man leaning over Buck. From the doorway, a lean, high-built puncher strode toward Buck, holstering a gun.

Then the older man looked up, still kneeling by Buck,

and this time he did not look at Tip, but to one side of him.

"What are you doing here?" he asked meagerly.

Tip shifted his glance, and then half caught his breath. It was a girl in a dry slicker who was climbing out from the tangle of chairs. She stood erect, catching hold of the back of a chair to steady herself, and on her neck Tip could see the livid bruise made by his fist when he swung in the dark. The girl didn't look at him, only looked at the man kneeling beside Buck.

"I was trying to bring this stranger a gun," she said calmly, no fear in her voice. "I've seen this happen too many times to like it, Hagen."

She glanced briefly at Tip. In that movement the coils of auburn hair lighted up in the play of the lamp shadows. Her face was pale, unnaturally so, and the lips of her wide and friendly mouth were drained of color. Only her eyes, of a cool gray, denied that she was scared and admitted that she was hurt. Her slicker, open now, revealed a blue basque, full at the breast, and a slim waist, belted with some material which held a six-gun.

Hagen Shields looked wickedly at her and then shifted his glance to Tip. "You hit him."

"To get him down!" Tip countered harshly. "I'm the second person in this town that doesn't like murder."

Hagen Shields rose, the other two on either side of him. "If that's so, I'm obliged. But obliged or not, you'll get out of this town."

To the tall puncher, who must have been Cam, Hagen Shields said, "Lug him out the back. Don't come till I tell you to." He strode out the alley door of the saloon, silent a moment, then called, "All right."

Neither of the remaining two spoke or looked at Tip or the girl. They carried the slack figure of Buck, a welt of blood glistening on his temple, out the door into the rain. It was as if they had forgotten Tip.

Tip watched them go and then turned to the girl. "I'm sorry about that. I was a little wild, I reckon."

The girl laughed shakily, in a low voice. "So was I. I don't blame you."

Tip walked over to her, bent down, and looked at her throat. She watched him with a kind of reserved suspicion in her eyes until she saw the concern in his face. She pulled her slicker collar up. "It hurts, but it'll go away."

"I—I didn't know you were in the room," Tip said humbly.

"How could you?" She looked over the room, and a weary disgust came over her face. Tip handed her out over the tangle of chairs, and followed her into the dark lobby. He waited while she lighted the lamp on the deal desk.

Only now anger was having its way with Tip. His eyes were wicked with it as he looked at the girl.

"I'm not going to like this town," he said quietly. "What did I walk into?"

"Buck Shields's yearly drunk," the girl answered calmly. "The Bollings wait for it, and always make a try for him. Buck gets disgusted every so often. He was ugly enough this time to drive his family away from him. That's when the Bollings made the try."

"Plain murder," Tip murmured, watching her.

The girl shrugged. "Hagen Shields would have done it to a Bolling." Then she added quietly, "Now will you go?"

"You, too?"

The girl nodded. "It's no threat this time, or no more than you've seen already. Last week they killed a whisky drummer out there in the street. He lay there for three hours, because this town is afraid. Can you understand that? Afraid to help a man!" Her eyes were dark with anger and contempt.

"But you're not," Tip pointed out.

"Once, no. Twice, yes. A man who stops here when he can ride around it is a fool, and you don't look like a fool!"

Tip walked over to the desk, opened the canvas-back register, took the pen from its glass of buckshot, and wrote his name in the book. It was not a brag; it was the only way of showing this girl without arguing that he was going to stay. Putting down the pen, he looked up at her. "Do I pay you?"

"You're going to stay?" she asked unconcernedly.

Tip nodded.

She looked at him, puzzled for the moment, then said in her quiet voice, "All right. Come along." She led the way up the dark stairway and down the corridor to the first door. She knocked, was answered, and said, "Wait, please," to Tip. As the door opened, he had a brief glimpse of a girl, face in hands, sitting on a chair beside a bed which held a gaunt, white-haired old man. When the girl stepped through the doorway, it was a picture that Tip would never forget. The blond girl sprang out of her chair, her face wild with fear, and said in a choked voice, "Did they get him, Lynn?"

Lynn, starting to close the door behind her, shook her head, and with a wild cry of relief the other girl was in her arms, great sobs wracking her body. The door, which Lynn had meant to close, remained open a few inches, and Tip settled slowly back against the wall. Lynn? Lynn Mayfell? Blackie Mayfell's girl?

And above the sobbing, Tip heard her speak to the other girl. It was spoken softly, with undertones of bitterness.

"Your dad's men will get him another time, Anna. Can't you understand that? They'll get him next time." Then, "Oh, darling, I don't mean to be cruel, but it's true!"

A man's voice, deep and rumbling and sick, said, "Did they wreck the place, Lynn?"

There was silence, and Tip could imagine her nodding. Then Lynn said, "There's a man here wants a room."

"What man?" the man asked.

"A stranger."

"Tell him we're full."

"It won't work, Uncle Dave. He knows, and he was in that fight, and he's stubborn."

There was a long silence, in which the sobbing died out. Then the old man said, "Ain't seven made up? Sure. All right, show him that."

Tip stepped away from the door, and Lynn Mayfell came out. She went down the hall, and he swung in beside her. At one of the doors, she paused and entered, striking a match on her boot. After lighting the lamp, she looked around and, satisfied, said coolly enough, "Good night."

"No key?" Tip inquired mildly.

She looked him full in the eye, and Tip could not tell if it was malicious pleasure he saw there. "No key," she echoed. "They don't do any good. Nobody steals anything, because there are no guests. And when they want in your room at night, they batter the door down. At least," she finished quietly, "they always have."

Tip grinned faintly. "Thank you, Miss Mayfell."

It was as if he had struck her across the face. For a moment Tip thought she was going to faint. Then she ran to the door, closed it, and leaned against it, stark fear in her face.

"Why—did you call me that?"

"It's your name, isn't it?" Tip asked, puzzled.

"No, no! It's Lynn Stevens. I tell you, it's Lynn Stevens!"

Tip walked across to her and faced her, his bony face curious.

"You're afraid. Of what? That pack of gun hands?"

Lynn said softly, "How did you know?"

"I'm huntin' your father's killer, miss. So are you, aren't you?"

"You've got to go!" Lynn said swiftly. "Last month a marshal came in here after the same thing. He was found dead! Don't you see? They'll get you!"

"And what about you?"

"They don't suspect me. And I can do more—a thousand times more than you! Don't you see—you'll spoil it! Spoil everything I've done!"

Tip shook his head, not answering.

"Will you go?" Lynn asked.

Again Tip shook his head. A kind of terror-driven hardness crept into Lynn's face. "If you don't, I'll tell them you're a marshal!"

"Go ahead," Tip said quietly.

She stared at him, then put her hand to mouth. "Oh, you fool, you blind, blundering fool!" she said softly. She went out, leaving Tip standing there frowning.

CHAPTER

3

TIP WENT TO SLEEP thinking about what Lynn Mayfell had told him, and he woke thinking of it. Only in the morning his mind was made up. The rain still held, and thin wisps of low clouds floated over the street, riding on a raw, driving wind out of the north.

There was nobody at the desk when Tip came downstairs. A glance at the saloon revealed a middle-aged pasty-faced man lackadaisically cleaning up the wreckage of yesterday evening. He glanced sourly at Tip and didn't speak as Tip retrieved his slicker from the bar top.

At the Oriental Café, a cubbyhole of a place run by a Chinaman, Tip wolfed down his breakfast in silence. It seemed to him that the grinning Chinaman, with his affable gibberish, was the first friendly soul he had met in Hagen. Afterward, having inquired directions, he set out in the rain, his slicker collar up, the raw rain in his face. Across the narrow mire of a street, in mid-block, he saw the weathered sign across the front of a shabby building: *Hagen Inquirer*. It brought a faint smile to his face. He crossed the street, the mud sucking at his boots, and came up on the boardwalk in front of a two-story building, long and narrow. Its upper windows were barred, but it was barren of any legend on the ground-floor windows or door. This, the Chinaman said, was the courthouse.

Tip stepped inside, stomping the mud from his boots on the sill, then looked up to confront two men. One of them wore a carefully pressed black suit and he was standing. The other was seated at a roll-top desk, and on his vest was the badge of the sheriff's office.

"Mornin'," Tip said cheerfully.

"This is a private conversation," Sheriff Harvey Ball

said flatly. He made no move to rise and it was plainly written on his harried face that he was a hostile man by nature. That he was past middle age was evident, in spite of the luxurious black mustaches amply bisecting his face. A pair of hard shoe-button eyes under thick brows, black as crow's wings, glared at Tip. The other man had a high-colored, squarish face as shrewd as an Indian's.

Tip said, "I said good mornin'."

"And I said this is a private conversation!" Sheriff Ball repeated irritably.

Tip sat down on a straight-backed chair and held his dripping Stetson between his legs. "It ain't any more," he said with mild truculence.

The three of them stared levelly at each other, and then Sheriff Ball said hotly, "Will you get out of here, mister?"

"No." Tip grinned faintly, challenging them both.

It was the man in the black suit who moved first. He said, "I'll be back later."

"No. I'll stop in at the bank later, Joerns."

Joerns went out, and Tip sat there while Ball swung around to face him. "Now what do you want?" Ball said bluntly, unpleasantly.

"Help."

"You won't get it from me. On what?"

"A friend of mine came in here last spring, Sheriff. Two months later his body was found about six miles out on the south road."

"You mean Blackie Mayfell, that prospector?"

Tip nodded.

The sheriff said, "Well?"

"What happened to him?"

"He was shot in the back."

"I read that," Tip said. "I wondered who shot him and why?"

"If I knew I'd arrest him," Sheriff Ball said bluntly.

And that, Tip thought, *is the first lie you've told me.* He said aloud, pacifically, "But you must have some idea."

Sheriff Ball's eyes were plainly hostile now. "And if I

have, can you give me a good reason for telling you?"

Tip's temper was edging him, but he kept his voice unruffled. "No. I was just Blackie's friend, that's all."

"There's been a man in here who wasn't even Blackie's friend and he wanted to know, too," Ball said meagerly.

Tip looked levelly at him. "I heard about him, too."

"Then you better think awhile about what happened to him," Ball said belligerently.

Tip said quietly, "Is that a threat?"

"Yes," Ball said immediately. He leaned forward a little, his eyes bleak. "There's no law in this county says I have to invite marshals in here to snoop. There's no law here says I got to give them any help. And I never asked for help." He leaned back. "We get along all right here. I was elected to office to carry out the will of the people."

"And that lets you stand by and let six men try to kill a drunk not a block from your office."

Surprisingly enough, the sheriff answered without heat, "Yes. That appears to be the will of my constituents."

Tip stood up. "Then everything I find out about Blackie's killer, I have to dig up myself?"

"That's right." The sheriff hesitated, then added mildly, "Only don't dig, mister."

Tip smiled faintly. "You know, I'm not a marshal, Sheriff, but I've run onto towns like this before—little towns cut off from the rest of the country. They think they're tough around here, a pack of hard-scrabble cowmen feudin' between themselves. But let a down-country hardcase drift in, a man a little handy with a gun, and that don't scare easy, and you'd be surprised at what big tracks he can make."

Ball's eyes glinted coldly. "You're the hardcase, eh?"

"Well, I come from down-country," Tip said gently. "Figure it out."

"We'll see," Ball said.

"You and a lot of other folks," Tip murmured. He stepped out into the rain and headed upstreet, not feeling anger so much as contempt. Whose man was Ball—the

Bollings' or the Shieldses'? And how was a man to get his teeth into this business, if a sheriff was afraid to talk? He passed the *Inquirer* office, glancing obliquely at its dusty window, and then halted suddenly, staring at the sign. He backtracked, after a moment's pause, and went inside.

A wooden railing separated the press shop from the editorial office, which consisted of a rickety desk, three chairs stacked with books and papers, and an overflowing wastebasket. A lamp was lighted over the job press, where a printer was turning out handbills. Beyond was the gloom of the press, and beyond it in the rear another lamp was lighted.

The man sitting at the front desk was a spare, dry man, and he looked over iron-rimmed spectacles at Tip, who tramped up to his desk, put both hands on the desk top, and said mildly, "I'd like some information."

The seated man blinked a little and cleared his throat and said, "All right."

"Where can I go to buy any information about the murder of Blackie Mayfell last spring?"

A subtle change came over the man's face. He said, "There's just two things I don't talk about in this town, mister. Just two names I don't print in my paper. One is Shields, and the other is Bolling."

"I'm not asking about them," Tip said.

"You are," the man said, "only maybe you don't know it. There hasn't been anyone shot in the back in this country that didn't take sides. And he took either the Shields side or the Bolling."

Tip lounged erect, his face impassive. "Can I put an ad in this paper?"

"That's what it's for. What kind of an ad?"

"An offer of a hundred dollars to anyone bringin' me information as to how Blackie Mayfell met his death."

The editor leaned back in his chair. "I hate to rob you," he said mildly. "Nobody will bite."

"I'll take the chance if you'll print it."

The editor pointed to the light in the back of the shop.

"They'll take your ad back there. The paper is out this afternoon."

Tip walked through the low gate, past the job press, past the type cases and the press, and came to an abrupt halt.

The girl reading proof at a low desk against the back wall was Lynn Mayfell. She looked up at his approach, momentary surprise on her face. Then she said quickly, in a low voice, "Remember my name is Stevens."

Tip nodded.

"What do you want?" she asked.

"I want to put an ad in this week's paper. Get your pencil."

She got a clean sheet of paper and poised her pencil over it, eyeing Tip inquiringly. She was very pretty, Tip noticed—lovely and angry.

"Head it 'Reward,' " Tip said, and went on dictating. " 'The undersigned will pay one hundred dollars cash to anyone bringing me information that leads to the arrest and conviction of the man or men who killed Blackie Mayfell last spring.' Sign it 'Tip Woodring.' "

The girl ceased writing and, still looking at what she had written, said, "I wouldn't do this," in a low voice.

"I know you wouldn't," Tip said stubbornly. "All I want is some information. Maybe you'd like to give me some?"

"I wouldn't," she said steadily. "And you won't get it this way. All you'll get is trouble."

She looked up at him, her face worried, and Tip said unsmilingly, "That'll keep me busy then until some information comes along. How much is it?"

"You're sure you want me to run it?"

"If you're not afraid," Tip said dryly.

Lynn coldly told him how much it was, and he paid and went out. That made three people who wouldn't talk, who were afraid to talk—Lynn Mayfell, the editor, and Ball, the sheriff. He'd give the town this one more chance. If nobody came in answer to his reward notice, then he would go after them. He didn't know how, but he was going to.

At the feed stable, he got his chestnut and rode out down the canyon south.

After five miles or so, the canyon spread out into a long, grassy park bisected by a creek that had cut in from the mountains to the east. It was a cheerless place in this rain, with the evergreens dark and foreboding. The red trunks of the jack pines were the only color here, those and the fat whitefaces grazing along the creek. Later, where a plank bridge spanned the stream close to a bottleneck in the park, Tip had his choice of two roads, and he chose to go straight on.

At the bottleneck, the timber crawled down almost to the stream, and the road, a clayey mire, swerved toward the stream.

Tip had been traveling the rain-soaked grass but now he pulled his horse into the road and slogged around the bend. The view from there was a spacious sweep of timber-stippled valley, broad and long, with curtains of rain obscuring the whole view.

His horse suddenly shied, and Tip pulled him up, looking around. Buck Shields, a rifle slacked across his saddle, was pulled just off the road into the edge of the trees.

He and Tip regarded each other in silence, and finally Buck spoke. "The road ain't public from here on."

Tip folded his arms and leaned on his saddle horn, the slow rain pelting his back. "I've been wonderin' about that all day," he observed tranquilly. He gestured toward the valley ahead. "This is the Shields country, then."

Buck nodded. Suspicion seemed to be warring eternally with the good nature apparent in his face. But it was a strong face, swart, almost heavy, and certainly stubborn.

"What country do the Bollings claim?"

"You passed the road across the bridge," Buck said flatly. "They're in a string of *cienegas* up in higher country." He was studying Tip, as if he were trying to place his face.

Tip smiled faintly. "Remember any of it?"

Buck's thick hand rose toward his temple, and halfway there, he checked the gesture. "Some," he said. "You hit me."

"I had to get you down."

Buck looked at him a long time. "Thanks," he said finally.

Tip said quietly, "I did you a favor, Shields. I'm going to claim one in return."

Buck said nothing.

"Blackie Mayfell was a friend of mine," Tip went on. He was going to continue, but he decided he'd let it go at that.

Buck didn't say anything.

Tip said, "I'm going to find out who killed him. All I know now is that he was found on this road."

Buck said, "Then you know about all there is to know."

"Not everything."

"All you will know," Buck amended.

Tip regarded him thoughtfully. Here it was again, the same hostile silence. But of all the people he had seen here thus far, Buck Shields, human enough to get drunk, sick enough of this mess to turn on his own kin when he was drunk, reckless and foolish enough to dare the Bollings to take him, fair enough not to shoot a stranger who walked up to him in a tight spot, seemed the most vulnerable man for what Tip planned.

Tip shifted in his saddle and said, "Not all I will know, either. For instance, it's a damn funny thing that Blackie was found on the only stretch of road that's open to everybody around here." He paused, wanting to isolate this, wanting it to jar Buck. "It's even funnier that a Shields put him there."

Tip was guessing. If he was wrong, Buck Shields's expression would tell him, so he could put the same question to one of the Bollings. If he was right, Buck would give it away, and with great care he watched Buck's face now. Because a man can't entirely mask surprise, Buck's face altered slightly, but the anger that came into it was not swift enough to serve as a protest of innocence. Tip saw Buck's big fist take a stronger grasp on his rifle.

"Whoever told you that is a liar," Buck said flatly. Somehow the statement lacked conviction and sounded curiously as if he were talking to fortify a spurious anger.

Tip felt a small elation. He pulled his horse around, lifted his reins, and said, "I'm not a marshal, Shields, but I'll bust this countryside open unless somebody talks. In two more days I'm going to the sheriff with what I know. If he won't help me, I'll do it myself. Think it over."

Buck watched Tip disappear around the bend, and even when Tip was gone he didn't move. Presently he put his horse down onto the road, walked him over to the bend, and thoughtfully watched Tip's disappearing figure.

Then he pulled his horse around and set off at a long lope across the park, heading south.

The Bridle Bit was a one-story sprawling log affair squatting on the edge of the timber. Caution or foresight had caused the barns and corrals to be built away from the timber, as if the Shieldses placed less importance on their own safety than they did on that of their possessions. The peeled logs, a deep red in this rain, were huge; five of them made a wall. A roofed passageway joined the biggest sod-roofed house with a smaller one, the cookshack. Behind it and at right angles was another house, what had been the bunkhouse in the days when the Shields herds were big enough to warrant riders.

Buck rode up to the corral, slipped the saddle off, turned his horse in, went over to the shed, and slung his saddle on a bar, then started for the house at a trot.

A movement by the high barn caught his attention, and he swerved his course. His uncle, Hagen Shields, had a spring wagon up on blocks in front of the open barn door, and he was greasing the hubs. His rifle lay within reach, propped against the loft underpinnings. He wiped his hands on a wisp of hay as he saw Buck coming toward him. Paused there, watching Buck, he was a hard-looking man, with implacability written all over his face. Even his Stetson, greasy and battered, rode his head at an uncompromising angle.

Buck pulled up short and walked into the barn.

"I just met this stranger down at the line."

"Coming here?" Hagen Shields asked.

"I dunno. But he knows," Buck said simply.

His uncle's face didn't change. "What did he say?"

"He asked me who killed Mayfell. I told him to find out somewhere else." Buck looked squarely at the older man then. "He said he knew a Shields put Mayfell's body out there on the road."

"He's guessing," the older Shields said. "Nobody saw you."

"Guessing or not," Buck said, his voice rising, "he's right. That's all Ball needs."

Hagen Shields studied Buck with bitter contempt in his eyes. "You're not going to cry, are you?"

Buck said warningly, "Careful what you say, Haig." His face was pale, and his thick-muscled fists were knotted.

Hagen Shields turned around and picked up another wisp of hay, aware that Buck's hot eyes were on him and superbly indifferent to the fact. "What I can't understand," he said gently, with irony in his tone, "is why you're afraid of something you didn't do." His eyes flicked to Buck. "Or did you?"

He seemed unaware of Buck's anger, because he went on in the same iron voice. "When you found that old desert rat dead, you told me yourself there was every sign that he'd been dumped on our land. I told you who dumped him there. I even told you to dump him back. But you knew better." His lip lifted in contempt. "You were a wrong-guesser, Buck. No, you weren't. I'll change that. You were soft."

Buck took a step toward him. The older man didn't move. He just stared at Buck, and presently Buck's eyes shifted.

"You can get drunk in town," the older Shields went on

implacably. "That's a normal risk an old man has to take on a young man, Buck. But don't ever try to be fair again to any Bolling."

Buck said miserably, "What about Ball?"

"If he knows, then he'll swing in with them. It's the hole he's needed and he'll crawl into it." He laughed shortly, without humor. "If you'd put that old man off the trail on one of the Three B *cienegas* where the roundup crew would have found him, then Ball would have been on our side, Buck." He looked thoughtfully at Buck. "You think he would have been any help?"

"No. But he's got the law behind him."

"Wrong," Hagen Shields said sparely. "There's no law here, Buck."

Buck watched him, getting some kind of strength from the older man's quiet confidence. Hagen Shields continued, his voice musing. "But I wouldn't let this stranger get to Ball with his hunch."

Buck's face altered, an expression of grim determination coming to it. "No, I won't do that, Haig."

"Suit yourself. It'll have to be done sooner or later. He's a troublemaker."

He went back to the wagon, dismissing Buck, who hesitated a moment, then tramped across the yard to the house.

At his entry into the kitchen, a girl, kneeling before the oven door with pans of bread in her hands, looked at him and said, "Hello," and went back to her work.

Buck paused in the middle of the room. A large table flanked by five chairs abutted the inside wall. The kitchen smelled of yeast, and it made Buck suddenly hungry.

"Where's Pate, sis?"

Lucy Shields rose and brushed a wisp of black hair from her forehead. She was a pleasant-faced girl, strong-looking, with violet-blue eyes and a full-lipped mouth, and with a kind of black Irish impudence in her uptilted nose, her round face. She looked at her brother and instead of answering him, asked, "What's the matter, Buck? What's happened?"

Buck hesitated a moment, then said gloomily, "This stranger at the fight, yesterday. He knows about me leaving Mayfell's body on the road."

Lucy wiped her hands on her apron, never taking her glance from Buck. Brother and sister looked at each other in eloquent silence.

"What are you going to do?"

Buck wheeled away to stand before the open door. "I don't know," he answered in a low, bitter voice.

"Buck."

Buck turned.

"Get out of here!" Lucy said swiftly. "I've asked you a hundred times before, but now even you can see what will happen. Take Pate and get out of here!"

"And leave you to face the music? No." Buck's voice was sullenly stubborn.

"I can face any music Haig or Cam can play!" Lucy said passionately. "It'll just be a year or so, Buck! Then they'll be dead, and I'll come to you and Pate. Please!"

Buck shook his head stubbornly, looking out at the rain. "No. The Bollings got Dad and they got Dave and they got Tom. I don't care about the others only I can't go away after that."

"But they're dead, Buck!" Lucy pleaded. "It wasn't your fight! If Uncle Haig hadn't come, it would only be memory." She paused, but Buck showed no inclination to reply. "Think of Pate, then, if you won't think of yourself. He's just a kid, Buck, and we're raising him to be a killer. He's out there now with a rifle, hunting men when he ought to be shooting squirrels. Think of it, Buck!"

"Stop it, sis!" Buck said sternly, wrath in his voice. More gently he added, "There's no turning back now."

"Not for men," Lucy said bitterly. "Not for fools!"

She went back to her work, and Buck still stood in the doorway. From there, he could watch Hagen Shields, slow and methodical, finishing his job. A sudden hatred for his uncle welled up in Buck. He was always wise, always right, as if his hatred for the Bollings had endowed him with a kind of omniscience. In another time, another place, Hagen Shields would have been a man to admire. Certainly his resourcefulness, his courage, and his implacability had kept them alive these last years. Buck remembered his conduct in the saloon yesterday as an example, and he hated Hagen Shields for saving him. Buck was too young to live with a monomania, as Hagen Shields did, talking hate, eating hate, thinking hate, planning revenge with a cunning and tireless clearheadedness. And now his uncle wanted him to kill this stranger.

Buck turned away, misery on his face, and saw that Lucy had been watching him.

"What is it, Buck?"

"I hate that man," Buck said in a voice trembling with anger and loathing. Lucy said nothing, and Buck knew that she hated him, too.

Suddenly Buck said, "Hagen says we've got to get that stranger. I wouldn't do it. He'll do it himself, now."

"Of course."

"But why? Why?"

The iron voice spoke from the doorway. "Because if you don't get him before he gets to Ball, Buck, then Ball will climb off his fence onto the Bolling side. He'll ask and get help from the marshal's office against us. And we'll go down."

Buck wheeled and went into the other room.

Hagen Shields smiled faintly at his disappearing back, then turned to Lucy. "Pour some hot water, Lucy. I'd like to wash my hands."

CHAPTER
4

Tip WENT BACK TOWARD HAGEN as far as the plank bridge spanning the creek. Across there, so Buck had said, lay the Three B, the Bolling outfit. He wondered if there was a rider pulled back there in the trees, watching him. He wondered, too, about the Bollings. How many of them were there, and what were they like?

He came to a sudden decision and crossed the bridge, angling off toward the timber. Achieving it unmolested, he went on. In early afternoon, having kept off the road, he came onto a high mountain pasture. Set in dead center of it and barren of any surrounding trees, was the Three B. Smoke from its chimney lay in a low blanket above the main house, a huge two-story log affair with a closed gallery running its length. It looked to be a big place, surrounded by two barns and a tangle of corrals and sheds. Two fenced pastures behind the barn held many horses. Tip could hear the faint sound of hammering from one of the sheds.

He was about to pull back into the timber when he heard the sound of horses slogging up the road a couple of hundred yards away. Dismounting, he held his hand over his chestnut's nose and watched the road. Presently two horsemen came into sight. One of them was leading a third horse, and this horse was dragging a travois such as the Indians use. Two poles, tied on either side of the saddle and joined by a crossbar behind the horse, were dragging on the ground. Between the crossbar and the ground end of the poles, a rough sort of stretcher had been shaped from blankets. And on this stretcher lay a man, a yellow slicker lashed over him. They passed the edge of the timber in silence, heading toward the house. Tip guessed that the fight in town yesterday had resulted in this casualty, and wondered if the Shieldses knew it.

He stepped into the saddle and swung back into the timber, heading again for Hagen. In two or three days, if his reward brought no information, he would visit this place again.

It was dark when he rode into Hagen, and the rain had stopped. There were people on the streets tonight, and more of the stores were lighted than had been last night, perhaps because the town had been forewarned then of the fight that was to take place. The same hostler took his horse, and this time he did not speak. But he studied Tip covertly as he went out, and Tip knew that the word had got around.

Passing the Mountain saloon, he saw that the broken windows had been boarded up. There was a murmur of conversation inside, and Tip went in. A dozen men were congregated at the poker tables and the bar, and they eyed him silently as he walked over to the bar. The conversation ceased as if cut off with a knife.

Tip said, "Whisky," and studied the room in the remaining large shard of the bar mirror. Slowly the talking was resumed, and this time there was low laughter mingled with it. Men couldn't laugh and fight at the same time, and Tip relaxed, reaching for the fresh newspaper that lay on the bar top. It was the Hagen *Inquirer* out that afternoon, and he folded it out flat and turned the page. On page two, in bold type, boxed in a heavy black border, was his reward notice. It was two columns wide and four inches deep and was off by itself, startling in its isolation.

Tip began to read it. Suddenly he paused and stared. The notice read: *The Undersigned Will Pay $1.00 Cash—*

Tip looked at it carefully. Yes, there was the period that had changed the one hundred dollars into one dollar. He felt his face flush hotly, and immediately memory went back to the scene in the *Inquirer* office. "I don't think it is wise," Lynn Mayfell had said. "I wouldn't do that if I were you." He had no need to look further for the reason for the misprint. Lynn Mayfell had purposely ordered it, and her aim was to accomplish a double·purpose. First, and most important, Tip suspected, was to make him ridiculous. Second, nobody in his right mind would sell valuable information for nothing, and a dollar was nothing for the risk involved. Suddenly, he began to understand the low laughter that had greeted his entrance.

A glance in the bar mirror revealed that he was still being watched. He saw three men break away from one of the poker tables and stroll toward the bar. Tip drank his whisky, composing his face, studying these men.

One of them, the leader, was a strapping man, barrel-chested, weather-bronzed, maybe fifty. He had the palest eyes Tip had ever seen, and they seemed to match his mustache, which was shades lighter than his skin and the color of weathered hay. He wore a suit of decent black, the coat of which hid crossed belts and a gun.

The second man was slighter, leaner, dressed in clean Levi's and faded denim jacket. The sharp planes of his face gave him a predatory look, and the rawhide-leanness of him backed up that impression. He was a beautiful machine designed solely for fighting, Tip reflected, and not like the third man, who was a heavy-boned, slow-moving man in need of a shave, a bath, and haircut. He had green eyes, the dirty, muddy kind that reminded Tip of slime on a pool.

It was the big man who stopped nearest to Tip. He had a bearing of power; his deep breathing, his slow movement, the smell of his pipe, the look of his big and capable hands as he placed them on the bar, the hulk of his big body, were quietly impressive, commanding.

He said, mildly enough, "You're Woodring, aren't you?"

Tip came erect. "Yes."

The man smiled slightly and put out a big hand. "My name's Ben Bolling." Tip shook hands with him, his face noncommittal. Bolling didn't bother to introduce the others. He gestured toward the paper. "You don't claim to be a spendthrift, do you?" His eyes were faintly amused.

Tip, remembering last night, bridled a little. "That's

just about what a dozen fancy lies will be worth, Bolling.
I'd only like to hear 'em."

Bolling's shrewd eyes were sizing him up. Bolling said,
"When can a man claim this reward?"

Tip murmured, "Right now." The whole room, including the sour-faced bartender, was listening.

"Let's see the money."

Tip took out a silver dollar and slapped it on the
counter.

"Hagen Shields killed Blackie Mayfell," Bolling said.
He turned to the lean puncher. "Am I right, Jeff?"

"We saw him," Jeff Bolling drawled. There was a glint
in his eye, but his face was as impassive as an Indian's. Tip
looked at him carefully, intently, feeling for what lay behind this.

Jeff Bolling went on. "It happened right here in this
saloon. Mayfell was standing here at the bar, his back to
the mirror." He paused dramatically, to see if Tip was
listening. He was, and Jeff continued.

"Me and Dad here, we stepped in from the lobby and
stopped in the doorway when we seen Hagen Shields at
that table over there playing solitaire."

Ben Bolling added gravely, "We didn't know what
would happen if Shields saw us, and we aimed to sneak
out."

Jeff Bolling took up the story, his Texas drawl slow and
steady. "But Hagen seen us in the bar mirror. He got rat-
tled, I reckon, because he drew his gun, but instead of
turnin' around to cut down on us, he shot at our reflection
in the bar mirror. He hit us, too."

"Don't tell me," Tip said. "I can guess it. He hit your
reflection, and you are so tough that the bullet bounced
off your reflection and hit Mayfell in the back and killed
him."

Jeff's face showed disappointment, but it didn't crack.
He said, in mock awe, "Son of a gun, you guessed it, mister!" just as the laughter broke out from his listeners.

Neither Ben nor Jeff nor Tip laughed, but just stood

there regarding each other. When the laughter subsided, Ben reached out for the silver dollar on the bar top, saying, "I guess that's what you wanted to know."

Tip's hand was there before his, covering the dollar. "Just a minute. Read the reward notice. The information has got to lead to the arrest of the killer, it says." He looked lazily at Ben Bolling. "Bring your story up to the sheriff and see if he'll believe it enough to swear out a warrant for Hagen Shields."

Bolling's face looked puzzled, expectant. Tip picked up the dollar and pocketed it. "If Ball will swear out the warrant leadin' to the arrest, the dollar is yours."

Ben Bolling's face darkened. He was about to speak when Jeff put a hand on his elbow. "Why not, Dad?" he asked softly. They looked at each other a brief moment, as if something unspoken were passing between them. Then Ben Bolling smiled.

"Why, sure. Come along," he said to Tip. To the puncher, he said, "You stay here, Murray."

The three of them, minus the unshaven puncher, went out and headed upstreet. Tip, still smarting under the jeering arrogance of the two Bollings, could not trust himself to speak. He kept telling himself to make no move until Ball showed his colors. If Ball listened to them, seemed to favor them, that was all that was necessary. After that, the Bollings could be taken care of, Tip thought grimly.

There was a light in the sheriff's office, and Tip went in first, Ben Bolling after him. The sheriff had his feet cocked up on the desk, and at sight of Tip and the two Bollings, he didn't move. A wary resentment crept into his face as he said, "Evening, gents."

He surveyed them all with impartial suspicion until Tip spoke. "I've got some information you might like to hear, Sheriff. These men say they saw Hagen Shields shoot Blackie Mayfell."

Ball's suspicious gaze shuttled to the Bollings. As before, their expressions were unreadable. Tip felt a wild desire to shake them out of that smug complacency, but he waited, calling on a patience he didn't know he had.

"That so?" Ball commented. He reached for a match on the desk, lighted the stinking four inches of cigar without burning his mustaches and imperturbably sucked it to life. In a way, Tip admired his gall. The sheriff said, "Why wasn't I told about this?"

"You never asked," Ben Bolling replied, his eyes challenging. "We're telling you now. Hagen Shields shot him in the back. We saw him."

Tip didn't offer the rest of the saloon story. He was interested in seeing what Ball was going to do. And intuition told him that the Bollings were seizing this opportunity to force Ball's hand, just as he himself was.

"You'd swear to that in court?" the sheriff asked.

"Sure," Jeff said.

"And you'll swear out a warrant for Hagen Shields's arrest?"

"I will," Tip put in.

The sheriff eyed him wickedly. "And you'll serve it, too, I suppose?"

"Not my job."

"Well, I can't serve it," Ball said flatly, uncomfortably.

Ben Bolling almost allowed himself a smile. "There's a way out of that, Harvey."

Ball looked at him blankly, saying nothing.

"Deputize somebody who will," Bolling went on, his voice prodding. "And if one man can't do it, deputize more. About ten, maybe."

"Your men?" Ball said dryly.

"There's only two kinds of men here. Shields's men and our men. And Shields's men won't serve a warrant on Shields himself. So I guess there's nothing left but to let us do it."

Ball said, "No."

"Think it over," Ben Bolling said. "You wouldn't want to make us mad."

Ball ignored him, looking at Tip. "I'm out of this fight.

I told you so today." He looked over at the Bollings. "That goes for you, too. I don't believe you saw Hagen Shields shoot him."

Tip, satisfied that Ball was not a Balling man and sick of watchnig Ball be bullied, murmured softly, "They didn't, Sheriff. Make 'em prove it."

Ball said irritably, "You keep out of this, Woodring!"

Jeff Bolling turned wicked, arrogant eyes on Tip. "That's good advice. Keep way the hell out of it."

Tip looked at the three of them, and he knew that something was going to happen and happen fast. The Bollings were talking his own brand of fight.

Ben Bolling said quietly, contemptuously, "I'll give you a half minute to get out of here, Woodring."

"And I'll give you ten seconds," Jeff amended.

Tip felt that cold gathering in his stomach, the feeling that he could not stop if he would. His left hand was on the desk top. Ball, feet still cocked on the desk, was eyeing him with malicious enjoyment.

Tip's right hand was at his side, and when it moved, it came up in one fluid motion, stopped a little above his hip, and his six-gun was nestled in his hand. With his left hand, he shoved the roll-top of the desk down, until it imprisoned Ball's feet. He swiveled his gun to cover the sheriff.

"You stay put, Sheriff," he drawled, taking a step toward Ball. The Bollings, wholly taken aback, backed up a step. Tip flipped the sheriff's gun out of its holster, leveled it at the Bollings, then kicked the sheriff's chair out from under him. Ball crashed to the floor on his back, the wind knocked out of him. Lying there on his back, his feet up and pinned at the ankles by the roll-top, he was helpless. Tip wanted him so.

He stepped up to Ben Bolling, flipped his gun onto the floor, and moved on to Jeff.

"That was a sucker play," Jeff said steadily. Tip didn't answer. Once the guns were on the floor, he threw open the door, and said to Jeff, "Kick them out."

Jeff hesitated only a moment, then kicked the guns out onto the sidewalk. Then Tip dropped his own guns out on the sidewalk, swung the door shut, and leaned against it, watching the look of puzzlement flush into Jeff's face.

"I was belly down behind the bar last night when you Bollings made your try," Tip said, his voice deceptively gentle. "I didn't like it then and I don't like it now, especially since I know you."

Jeff drawled insolently, "What do you aim to do about it, Red?"

Tip lashed out then, his fist catching Jeff Bolling full in the face. Jeff staggered back, caromed off Ben, and crashed into the desk, tripping over Ball, who had his arms up protecting his face. Ben Bolling reached for the chair. Tip, dodging his kick, sank a fist in his midriff. Ben doubled up, and Tip laced an uppercut into his face, driving him into Jeff who was just rising. They both went down again on top of Ball, who yelled in anger. Jeff was up first, fury in his face. Tip took his wild swing in the chest, and was knocked back against the door. Using it as a brace, he lunged at Jeff, beating down his guard. He caught him around the waist, lifted and heaved him into Ben. Again the two of them went down. This time Tip didn't wait for them to get up. He dove on Ben, slashing at his big head. The impact hurt his fist, shocked his arm clean to the shoulder. But he had driven Ben's head into the side of the desk, and he felt his body go slack under him. Tip whirled, half rising, to see Jeff, the chair raised over his head, rushing at him.

Tip dived at his feet as the chair whistled over his head and crashed into the floor, and Jeff went down. Grunting savagely, panting for breath, they grappled on the floor. Ball, calling futilely for help and cursing like a madman, rolled out of their way as best he could while they thrashed around the floor. Jeff had a strangle hold on Tip, and Tip had a palm against Jeff's chin. He pushed until the blood in his temples was ready to burst, and when he felt Jeff's hold slacking, he pushed harder. Suddenly Jeff's arms

slipped away. Tip rolled over, coming to his knees. Jeff
was just rising, too. They came erect facing each other,
slugging wildly, toe to toe, their grunting and the dull
smack of flesh on flesh the only sounds in the room. A kind
of wild anger had its way with Tip. He knew he was being
hurt and he didn't care. He knocked Jeff back against the
wall, and Jeff aimed a kick at his groin. Tip caught his
foot and twisted, and Jeff fell on Ball and rolled against
the wall. He came up in front of the side window and Tip
dived at him. His lunge caught Jeff off balance and they
crashed into the window. Tip heard the shower of glass,
the splinter of wood, and they were brought up short. Jeff
was bent backward half out the window, the weight of
Tip's body pinning him there. Tip kept it there, slugging
at Jeff's face. He drove blow after blow into Jeff's face
until his fists throbbed, and then he stepped away. Jeff
slacked into the room and rolled onto the floor. Tip
stepped back, waiting for him to move. He didn't.

A sudden sound drew Tip's attention. He looked
around to see Ben Bolling slowly, painfully, dragging himself to his feet. Tip helped him up, stood him erect, and
swung on him with every ounce of his nearly exhausted
strength. Big Ben Bolling crashed into the table and fell
on his back and did not move.

Tip stood there, his fists bloody, his shirt half torn off
him, dragging air into his lungs. A warm trickle of blood
flowed down his chin, and he scoured it off with the back
of his hand. He was suddenly aware that Ball, lying on
his back between the two down Bollings, feet still pinned
up under the roll-top, was quietly regarding him with his
owl eyes.

Tip said wickedly, "There's more where that came from,
Sheriff. You want loose?"

"No," Ball said softly. "No, thanks."

Tip picked up his Stetson, jammed it on his head, and
strode to the door. He paused there and said to Ball, "I'll
make bigger tracks than that, Ball, before I'm through
here," and went out.

He left the door open, and a moment's search revealed his gun on the boardwalk. He rammed it into his waistband and headed down street on unsteady legs. He felt burned out and tired, but his anger still prodded him when he thought of the Bollings and the arrogance with which they set about building the frame-up for Hagen Shields. He had no love for Shields, but to see two men solemnly swearing to a lie, a bullying, roughshod malice in their every act, was a little too much to take. He had made two enemies tonight who would either drive him out of the country or kill him, he knew.

He crossed the street and wearily dodged under the tie rail and mounted the other boardwalk. Where would he go now, and what could he do? His own temper had made this town an impossible place to stay. And he was no nearer the truth now than he had been yesterday. Somebody here knew something about Blackie Mayfell, else why did everybody refuse to talk about it? It wasn't all fear of the Shieldses or the Bollings.

He paused there in the half-darkness of the street, thinking. Lynn Mayfell knew something. Buck Shields knew something. A sudden memory of the old man in bed at the hotel, the man Lynn had talked to last night, came to Tip. This old man favored neither the Shieldses nor the Bollings, else he couldn't keep alive in this town. And he was close to Lynn Mayfell. Maybe he would talk.

Tip swung into the hotel lobby to find it deserted save for an old man behind the desk whom he had not seen before. The clerk stared at him, and Tip suddenly realized that he was not a pretty sight, and just as suddenly decided he didn't care. Mounting the stairs with dragging steps, he paused at the first door in the corridor, knocked, was bidden enter, and stepped inside.

Lynn Mayfell sat in the chair beside the bed. She rose as Tip closed the door behind him. They stared at each other a long moment, and Tip doffed his Stetson.

"What—what happened to you?" Lynn asked in a weak voice.

Tip said dryly, "I bought it all for one dollar. Does that sound familiar?"

A deep flush crept into Lynn's face.

"Go on," Tip prodded gently. "Tell me it was a mistake of the printer's."

"It wasn't!" Lynn said shortly. "I did it on purpose. I'm—very sorry if it got you in trouble."

Tip said unsmilingly, "No, you aren't sorry, lady. The more trouble comes my way, the better you like it." He looked at the old man in the bed, who was watching him with burning eyes. He had been a magnificent man once, Tip could see, before his body wasted away. His hair was thick, dead-white, his face pale to emaciation, and his hawklike nose was so thin and sharp that it was almost transparent. Tip walked up to him and said gently, "I'm Tip Woodring, old-timer. I'd like to ask a few questions from you, because you haven't got anything to lose by answering me, like"—he glanced coolly at Lynn—"some people around here."

"All right."

"I'm here to find out who killed Blackie Mayfell," Tip said. "They know about him around here, but they won't talk to a stranger. I figure they will talk if I take sides in this row. Who's right, the Shieldses or the Bollings?"

"Neither," Uncle Dave said bitterly. "They're both wrong as hell."

"Who do you favor?"

"I like Buck Shields, and I hate Hagen Shields," the old man said. "I like Lucy Shields and I hate Cam Shields, and nobody could help liking that poor kid, Pate. I like Anna Bolling, and she hates and I hate Jeff and Ben and Yace Bolling and every man that works for 'em, including Murray Seth, their foreman. About the people who take sides with either the Shieldses or the Bollings, they're buzzards. Ain't a one of 'em but hopes to get loot when the other side goes down." He looked at Tip. "That help you?"

"Some. What about Ball?"

Before the old man could answer, Tip heard the pounding of feet taking the stairs two at a time. Tip wheeled, drawing his gun, and said to Lynn, "Keep your head and there won't be trouble."

He went over to the door and flattened against the wall, just as a savage knock came on the door. Tip, glancing at the floor, saw the imprint of his own muddy tracks, and he knew that somebody had followed them to this room. Lynn made a move to come over to the door, and Tip shook his head and motioned her to stand there. Lynn stopped and said, "Come in."

The door flew open, and Tip, who was behind it, had to wait for the voice before he knew who it was. But when the man said in a tight voice, "Where is he?" Tip knew it was Jeff Bolling.

"Who?" Lynn asked calmly.

"That redhead! He's been here, because there's his tracks!"

Tip edged forward. Now he could see only Jeff's hand and wrist, and Jeff was holding a gun pointed at Lynn.

Tip, without a moment's hesitation, lashed at Jeff's wrist with his gun barrel. He heard the impact, saw the gun drop, and he stepped out to confront Jeff, whose bloodied and swollen face held a look of agony.

Tip balled up Jeff's shirt front in his fist, shoved him back through the door out into the hall, and then literally threw him down the stairs. He stood there watching Jeff land on his back halfway down the stairs, and turn a slow and complete somersault in the air before he crashed into the newel post, taking out a section of the rail with him. Jeff rolled to a stop, rose to an elbow, and yelled, "Go get him!"

Tip stepped back into the room, walked across it, shoved open the window, and said, "What's out there?"

"A twelve-foot drop to the saloon roof," the old man said, and then, surprisingly, he smiled. "Hole up in the loft at the stable, son. And be quick about it."

Tip swung out the window, just as the sound of running

feet below came through the open door. He had only a brief glimpse of Lynn, her mouth open in startled amazement. Halfway out the window, Tip hung there long enough to say to her, "It's taken you a long time to find out that a woman can be too closemouthed, hasn't it?" And then he dropped.

He was standing in the alley when he saw the shape of a man, a gun in each hand, lean out the second-story window of the hotel.

Tip smiled and faded down the alley into the night. At the rear entrance to the feed stable, he could look through the long centerway and see the hostler seated in a back-tilted chair under the front arch, a lantern on a nail over his head. Tip noiselessly swung up into the loft, pulled hay over himself, and dropped off to sleep.

He didn't know when it was that he wakened with the certain knowledge that there was somebody close to him. When he felt a hand on his shoulder, he lunged away, clawing at the gun in his waistband.

Then a woman's voice said, "Careful. Oh, please be careful!"

Tip was silent a moment. The loft was dark as pitch, and he couldn't even make out a figure. Yet he was sure it was not Lynn Mayfell who had spoken.

He whispered, "Who is it?"

There was a rustling in the hay, and suddenly he felt a hand touch him. Tense, he waited.

"Is it Tip Woodring?"

"Yes. Who are you?"

"It doesn't matter," the voice whispered. "I'm Lucy Shields. You've got to leave this country!"

"I've heard that before. Why do I?"

"Hagen Shields, my uncle, is going to kill you. I don't know how, but he intends to do it."

"What for?"

There was a pause. "I can't tell you. Only it's true."

Tip pondered that a moment, and then he said stubbornly, "I don't get it. Is this just a scare? You don't know me, and I don't know you, except your name is Shields. I know the Shieldses don't want me here, and I don't reckon I'll go because you say to."

"Please! You don't know my uncle. He'd—kill me if he knew I talked to you!"

"I won't tell him," Tip said.

"And you'll go?"

"No." There was a long pause, and he added, "Thanks for the help, though."

"You were kind to Buck once," she said. "I'm only trying to warn you that you're in danger."

Tip said, "Thanks again," and listened to the hay stirring. Presently he was alone in the dark. He sat there pondering the reason for this girl's visit, cursing himself for a suspicious fool. She meant well toward him. What had that old man said? Buck and Lucy and Pate he liked; Cam and Hagen, he hated.

Tip settled back into the hay. After tonight, he thought, he had chosen his side. Hagen or no Hagen, he was for the Shieldses.

CHAPTER
5

TIP SLEPT LATE. When he came awake, he was aware that the sun was shining, that it was a crisp fall day, that the hostler out in the corrals was whistling, and that he was hungry.

When he stretched, his very bones seemed to cry out in agony, and he discovered that he had only half the usual visibility in his right eye. He touched it gingerly, and felt other bruises.

Somebody walked down the centerway below him, and there were voices. Tip became still, listening.

It was Sheriff Ball, and he was saying, "For the thousandth time, Miss Stevens, I don't intend to arrest him. All I want is to talk to him."

"I don't believe you," Lynn said coldly. "I hope he shoots you."

"He probably will," Sheriff Ball said. "May I call now?"

"All right," Lynn said.

Ball called out, "Woodring! Tip Woodring!"

Tip peered over the edge of the loft. Ball saw him first. They regarded each other, Tip with suspicion in his face, Ball with curiosity.

Ball finally said, "I haven't got a gun. I want to talk to you. Come down here."

Lynn wheeled and watched Tip hit the floor. He was covered with hayseed; the blood on his face and on his swollen, cut hands was dried an ugly brown color. His right eye was tinged a purple, and his red hair was tousled. There was a kind of ingrained belligerence on his face that suddenly made Lynn Mayfell laugh.

Tip growled, "What's funny?" and then he grinned.

This girl had the most contagious laugh he had ever heard. As a matter of fact, he had never heard her laugh. His grin faded, however, when he saw the black-and-blue spot on her neck where he had hit her. He was still ashamed of that.

She nodded to Ball and said, "I guess my business is done."

"Thank you, Miss Stevens," Ball said. Erect, Ball was something of a banty rooster. He had a pouter-pigeon chest, and the effect was enhanced by his thick mustaches. He lifted his hat to Lynn, who nodded in a strangely friendly manner to Tip and went out.

Afterward Tip and Ball regarded each other without much to say. Finally, Ball said, "You look like hell."

"I feel like hell," Tip said. "Is that what you wanted to talk to me about?"

Ball's expression was one of long-suffering. "You know, I've seen and heard some hot tempers in my time, but never one like yours."

"If you think I'm going to tell you I'm sorry I shut that desk on you last night, I'm not."

"I know you're not," Ball said grimly. "Let's get some breakfast." When Tip still looked suspicious, Ball said, his voice pleading, "Look, son, all I want is a talk with you. Don't fly off the handle till you hear me out."

Tip said reluctantly, "All right." He nodded his head toward the street. "Is it safe out there?"

"The Bollings went home in a hired buckboard last night. As for the rest of the town, I think it will be glad to let you alone."

Tip said nothing, but fell in beside Ball. They stopped at the Oriental Café and ordered breakfast. Ball, friendly enough, was uncommunicative, and Tip couldn't guess what would follow. Finished eating, they stopped at Sig's Neutral Elite while Tip bought a new shirt, then they proceeded to the sheriff's office. It was a shambles, with one window out, the chair a pile of kindling, and one leg off the table. Calendars and reward dodgers were scattered over the floor, smeared with mud and blood.

Tip put on his clean shirt under Ball's contemplative eye, then took the swivel chair Ball offered. He sat down, a rather truculent-looking redhead, ready for and expecting the worst.

Ball cleared his throat and said, "That was a nice, tidy job you did last night. It needed doing."

Tip said carelessly, "You ought to know. They're your friends."

"They'll shoot on sight, from now on, of course."

Tip nodded, unimpressed.

Ball said placidly, "Lying on my back there last night until someone stepped in and lifted that roll-top off my feet, I saw a lot of things besides just the ceiling." He looked sideways at Tip.

"For instance."

"I saw that I'd got pulled into this fight by the scruff of my neck."

"On whose side?"

"Nobody's side," Ball said, shaking his head. "I've just decided I'm through bein' a tinhorn lawman. I'm goin' to try to fill my pants, from now on."

"Maybe."

Ball shrugged. "You ought to know, because it's goin' to depend on you."

Tip was suddenly alert. "Me?"

"Yes. I want you to take a deputy's badge, Woodring."

Tip's jaw slacked open in honest amazement, and he stared at Ball in utter disbelief.

"Wait a minute, before you shoot off your mouth," Ball said hurriedly. "I used to be something of a scrapper, Tip. I like a good fight. But I don't like a gang fight, and especially I don't like odds of twenty to one. So I've stayed clear of this row here. I've seen men murdered. I've seen them shot in the back, and I've seen them bushwhacked. And I've seen the misery and the suffering and grief it's caused." His voice was low, in dead earnest. "I've kept on the fence in this fight, because I was scared—just plain

scared. And it was useless to do anything else. I could have
tromped on either side a dozen times, but I'd have been
shot for my pains. Can you understand that?"

"Sure. It's natural, I reckon."

"It's me that sent for that marshal who was killed, Tip.
I sat in this office and cussed him to anybody who'd listen,
like I cussed him out to you. But I sent for him. And I
tried to help him—in secret. But it was no good. I kept
hopin' the commissioners would send me a git-down, cold-
steel, hell-for-leather fightin' man that I could take a risk
on. If I'd got a man like that, I would have throwed all
my weight behind him. I'd have come out in the open
and fought with him, takin' on all comers." He paused
and shook his head. "But all they sent me was just another
lawman—and he wasn't good enough."

He came off the table now and faced Tip, hands on hips.
"You are," he said simply. "You got a wild temper, and I
dunno why, but you seem to savvy this kind of fightin'.
They talk tough to you and you knock their teeth down
their throats. You're the kind of man I wanted, Tip. You
say you want to find Blackie Mayfell's murderer. Throw
in with me, and together we'll find him." He paused.
"Well, what about it?"

Tip was seeing Sheriff Ball in a new light. All the sour-
ness, the suspicion, the irritability, and the truculence
were gone from him. And Tip suspected that this Sheriff
Ball, the little wise man who hated murder, was the real
one.

Tip said, "One thing, Sheriff. Are you holdin' out information about Blackie Mayfell on me, hopin' to blackmail me into takin' this job?"

Sheriff Ball shook his head. "Blackie Mayfell was found
on that south road. That's the only blamed thing I can
tell you about the man."

Tip made up his mind then, quickly and definitely. "It's
a deal. How you goin' to start?"

Ball grinned under his mustache. It was a tight grin,
full of meaning. "They'll start it, one side or the other.

And it don't matter which starts. Whoever it is, we'll tromp on 'em. They'll find out there's a law in this country for decent people. They'll be decent, I reckon, or they'll die."

A half hour later, his deputy's badge in his pocket, Tip left the sheriff's office. At the *Inquirer,* he stepped inside. The editor was not there, but the pressman was working again at the job press. And in the rear against the back wall the overhead lamp was burning, and Lynn Mayfell, by its light, was at work proofreading tax notices.

Tip strolled up and took off his Stetson, smiling. Lynn almost smiled in reply, and leaned back in her chair.

"I haven't had a chance to thank you for last night," she said gravely.

"For what?"

"Well, after all, Jeff Bolling was pointing a gun at me."

Tip made a deprecatory gesture, but Lynn said quickly, "That's just your trouble, Tip. You take this all as a sort of brawling joke."

Tip said curiously, "You mean you think he'd have shot you, a woman?"

"There have been women hurt in this fight," Lynn said gravely. "You see, I understand it. And your way, the hottempered, reckless way, isn't going to help."

Tip put a leg on her desk and sat down, saying nothing.

Lynn, after a pause, went on. "I think you have the worst temper of any man I've ever known."

Tip's eyebrows rose, but he still kept silent.

Lynn laughed, a little embarrassed, and added, "Uncle Dave wants to see you again."

"Who is he?"

"He owns the hotel. He was here with the original Shields and the original Bolling. He's an old man, and a fair one—and he's going to die."

"Does he know who you are?"

Lynn nodded assent.

"And he knows what you know about your father's killer?" Tip asked gently.

Tip said curiously, "You know what your dad was after?"

"Of course I do," Lynn said angrily. "He had discovered gold, and a lot of it."

"And you don't think Buck would kill him to hide that? Or Hagen?"

"Hagen would, but Buck wouldn't!" Lynn banged a fist on the table. "Why don't you let me alone?" she cried. "I like Buck, and I know him, and you don't! Now I suppose you'll arrest him and lose whatever chance I've got of getting the truth from him."

Tip's face flushed a beet-red. "You know," he said thickly, "there's just one thing worse than a mule-headed woman, and that's two of 'em. No, I won't arrest your nice little Buck. You can get him drunk, like any honky-tonk girl, and find out what you damn well please. Good-by!"

Tip stalked past the press in a towering rage. There he paused, looked back at Lynn, and came back to her.

"I didn't mean that last," Tip said miserably. "But why do you rawhide a man so? Hell, I'm tryin' to help you if you'll let me. And I don't like this bullyin' any better than you do."

Lynn, tense as wire, suddenly relaxed. She said, "Maybe I deserved it. But I'm doing the best I can. And your way seems so clumsy, so brutal. You can't beat truth out of people, Tip."

"And you can't coax it out of them."

Lynn smiled. "Then I guess you'll have to go your way and I'll go mine. But—let's don't fight any more. And I'll give you any information I get if you'll give me yours."

"It's a deal," Tip said, and grinned suddenly. They shook hands on it, and Tip went out. This time, for a reason unknown to him, he was whistling.

Tip headed downstreet toward the barbershop opposite the Mountain saloon for a shave. With sudden gravity he realized that his period of indiscriminate hell-raising was over. There was a responsibility attached to wearing a law badge, one that did not allow for a hot temper. He had come here to uncover a murderer, and had wound up as a deputy, not much closer to the truth than the night he had come. Lynn's information as to Buck Shields meant nothing, for Tip believed as Lynn did, that Buck didn't do it. Nobody, it seemed, killed Blackie Mayfell, and yet he was dead with a bullet hole in his back.

About to turn into the barbershop, Tip glanced across the street. Hagen Shields and Buck were dismounting at the tie rail in front of the saloon. They went inside, and Tip stood there on the boardwalk, remembering what Lucy Shields had said last night. Normally, the sight of Hagen Shields would only serve as a reminder of that night in the saloon, the memory of which still rankled Tip. But added to what the girl had said last night, it was nothing short of a dare.

Tip crossed the street and entered the saloon. Buck and Hagen were at the bar, and Tip walked up to it, stopped next to them, and asked for a drink. He nodded to Buck, who nodded back and then left the bar for one of the poker tables, on which were scattered some papers. Hagen Shields, his face without expression, stared levelly at Tip and then away. Tip looked in the bar mirror at Buck, and found that Buck was watching him. Suddenly, Buck shook his head from side to side, saying no in as plain a manner as a man could without speaking, and he was saying it to Tip, for in front of Hagen the bar mirror was broken out.

Tip scowled, perplexed, and suddenly Buck cleared his throat.

"Woodring," he said firmly, "I see your ad here in the paper. You don't aim to leave, then?"

Tip waited until the bartender set the bottle and glass in front of him, poured his drink, then turned sideways and stared levelly at Buck. "No," he said flatly.

"I thought we told you the other night to light a shuck," Buck said. His voice was strained, and he stared intently at Tip. There was more worry in his eyes than threat or anger.

Tip asked curiously, "What are you tryin' to do, Shields?

Crowd me into a fight?"

Buck said in a voice that was near to cracking, "You can walk out that door and get on a horse, or you can go for your gun."

Tip stood motionless a second. He was beginning to understand this, now. Buck and Hagen were to separate when they saw him, then Buck was to make the fight talk. But Hagen, out of it apparently, would make the real play. Maybe Buck was trying to tell him, by that nod, that he didn't mean what he said, and trying to do it without Hagen seeing him.

Tip took a sudden decision in that second. He said in a soft voice, "Open the ball, then, Shields. I'll stay."

Buck's hand dropped to his gun. It wasn't a very fast movement, as if Buck were reluctant to do it. Tip's right hand dropped to his gun. And then, out of the corner of his eye, Tip saw Hagen Shields's hand streak to his hip. Tip still had the whisky bottle by the neck in his left hand. He brought it around in a swift looping arc that caught Hagen Shields on the side of the head. Shields staggered sideways, and Tip's gun whipped out and up and caught him squarely on the side of the head.

Before he hit the floor, Tip's gun was leveled at Buck, who, mouth open was watching this, his gun half clear of leather.

Tip said, "Drop that!"

Buck seemed glad to. Tip looked down at Hagen Shields. He was bleeding where the whisky bottle had crashed into his skull.

Tip stirred him with his toe and then said to Buck, "Pick him up and carry him to the jail, Shields. I want the whole town to see this."

He thought Buck was going to smile, but instead he came over, picked up his uncle, and hefted him up on his shoulder, like an oversize sack of feed.

They marched down the street that way, Buck sweating under his load, Tip beside and a little behind him. A small crowd gathered behind them, and some laughed. Tip thought it was a pity that Hagen Shields, that dignified and merciless man, couldn't hear that. But he would hear it at second hand.

Ball greeted them at the door. "Open up the cell block, Sheriff," Tip said. "Here's your first customer."

Tip helped Buck lug Hagen up the stairs and throw him into the cell. There were six cells in the block, roofed, floored, and walled on one side with heavy planks. It was not a break-proof jail, but a sturdy one. The rest of the second story was empty, except for a ladder that mounted to a padlocked door in the roof.

Hagen Shields came to rest on the cot, and then Buck pulled out his handkerchief and wiped his face. His grin at Tip was friendly.

"Thanks," he said. "I didn't know whether you savvied it."

"What was it all about?"

Buck said bitterly, "Haig had it fixed up to kill you, that's all. He was goin' to do it while you made your play for me."

"But what for?"

"You knew."

"Knew what?"

Buck looked quizzically from Tip to the sheriff, and then back to Tip. "You ain't told him?"

"Told him what?" Tip asked blankly.

Buck sighed. "Well, I might's well tell you the whole thing, Woodring. You see, after you accused us the other day of bein' the ones who left Blackie Mayfell on the south road and give me the deadline, Haig decided to get you before you got to Ball with your story." He paused. "You see, I really did put Mayfell there."

"Where'd you find him?"

"Up in our north pasture. He'd been dumped there, because I could see the tracks of the horses. I got panicked, I reckon, because I thought it was a Bolling frame-up. So I dumped him out on the south road." Buck stopped, watching Tip.

"What else, Buck?" Tip asked gently.

"That's all."

Tip smiled faintly and shook his head. "Buck, you don't look like a man that would take somethin' like that lyin' down. Maybe you did get scared and put Blackie's body off your land. But you weren't satisfied with that. You said there were tracks. You mean you didn't backtrack to see where they came from?"

Tip stopped talking, and Buck said nothing, only looked uncomfortable. Tip went on relentlessly. "I can tell you what you did, Buck. You trailed those horses back to where Blackie Mayfell was really murdered. And you saw something there that you don't want to believe. You're hidin' someone, Buck. Who is it? Cam or Hagen?"

"No," Buck said. "That's not true!"

Ball said gently, "It's part true, Buck. You can't hide it."

Buck wheeled away and walked to the corridor window that looked down on the street. There was an agony of indecision reflected in his face. Tip signed to Ball to keep quiet, and then he walked up to Buck.

"Do you like this feudin', Buck?"

"I hate it!" Buck said angrily, not looking at Tip.

"Ball and you and I are going to clear it up," Tip said quietly. "The man over there in that cell is one of three or four men who's kept it goin', Buck. He's in jail. There'll be others in jail, before we're done. But if you're goin' to work with us, we've got to have the truth—all the truth about Blackie Mayfell. Because I think we can use Blackie Mayfell's death to bust this wide open. What about it?"

Buck looked at him then, sudden hope in his eyes. "You and me and Ball?"

Tip nodded. "Of all the men in this fight, Buck, you're the only man who isn't a liar and who hates it. That's why we've picked on you for help. Are you goin' to string along with us?"

Buck came to a sudden decision. "If you want me."

"We want you, and what you can tell us, too."

Buck wiped the sweat from his forehead with his handkerchief and looked at Ball, who nodded assent. "All right," Buck said in a tight voice, "I'm tellin' the truth now, Woodring. I did backtrack those horses, trailed 'em deep onto Three B range until I come to the place where they'd picked up Blackie Mayfell. There was a lot of horse tracks there, and boot tracks—and other tracks. I found Blackie's tracks, and they was old. But there was one more set of tracks just as old as Blackie's. They"—he looked miserably at Tip—"was a woman's."

Tip was puzzled. Ball said, "Anna Bolling's, you mean?"

Buck nodded mutely. Ball coughed warningly and said, "You're sure of that, Buck?"

When Buck nodded again, Ball shook his head. "Hell, that don't mean anything, Buck."

"Of course it don't," Buck said quickly, apparently relieved, "only it don't look very good. Anna Bolling wouldn't hurt a fly," he stated positively, as if challenging them to deny it.

"She could have found him," Ball said.

"That's what I thought. Only I couldn't tell Haig or Cam because they'd have brought it to you, Sheriff. And maybe she—well, maybe she couldn't explain it, and they'd have crowded you into makin' trouble for her."

"I won't trouble her," Ball said gently. "Not that way."

Buck drew a deep sigh of relief. Tip, remembering the glimpse of Anna Bolling he'd had that first night, and recalling her words, thought he understood now. Buck was trying to be fair to a girl whose family he hated, torn between that and his loyalty to his own. And something else, too.

Buck said gently, "She's the only Bolling alive that wouldn't like to see all us Shieldses dead." He laughed shortly. "Well, maybe we will be, now that Haig's put away."

"Why?" Tip asked.

"Because when they hear about it, they'll raid us. They're afraid of Haig, but not of Cam or me or the others."

Ball said grimly, "Maybe we can arrange a little reception for them, Buck."

Buck only smiled his relief. Tip found himself liking him, wondering how a man could go through what Buck had been through and still remain fair and considerate. They tramped down into the office, Ball asking Buck questions, Buck answering them. There was none of the old hostility between them, and Tip knew that today the Vermilion feud had changed its course, and for the better.

But the death of Blackie Mayfell was still a mystery—and likely to remain so. For Buck didn't believe Anna Bolling killed Blackie, didn't believe she could tell him much, even if she would. And she wouldn't talk, he was certain. Why would she, when her brothers hated him and had sworn to kill him? And they would hate him a lot more before he was through with them, Tip thought somberly as he tramped downstairs behind the sheriff and Buck. A lot more.

CHAPTER
6

ANNA BOLLING WALKED OUT to Dr. Pendexter's buggy with him. Complete quiet had fallen on the place, a quiet which she dreaded. Dr. Pendexter put his black bag in the buggy and turned his sad face toward her. He was a mussed little man, gloomy and friendly and expert.

"I'm sorry, girl," he said. "If they'd brought him to me after it happened, he might have had a chance." He shook his head. "But hauling him all that way in the rain, and not even in a wagon."

Anna bit her lip, shivering. She had slipped on a man's coat to come out with the doctor, and now she hugged herself against the brisk wind driving off the mountains. Today the sun didn't seem to warm anything, and she shivered. Small strands of corn-colored hair whipped into her face, and she was oblivious to it.

Dr. Pendexter put a hand on her arm. "Why don't you move away from it, Anna?"

Anna said dully, "Oh, it doesn't matter. Moving away wouldn't stop it, and I'd rather be here if it has to happen."

The doctor eyed her frankly. "Yace was the best of the lot, and now you haven't even got him. It won't be easy."

"It never was."

Dr. Pendexter sighed. "Well, Yace is gone, and Hagen Shields is in jail. The Shieldses and the Bollings will be an extinct breed in another year."

Anna asked curiously, "Hagen Shields in jail? Was it for murdering Yace?"

The doctor shrugged. "I don't follow it, girl. I try to forget it."

Anna nodded and watched the doctor climb into the buggy and pick up the reins. He said gloomily, "If you're going to stick it out, I suppose I can't change your mind." He pointed with his buggy whip across the park to a pair of tall cottonwoods on the edge of the evergreen timber. At this distance, they could only see a tiny figure at work, but they both knew he was digging a fresh grave in the Bolling graveyard, which already held most of the family. "When it's filled up, girl, you'll have given the best years of your life to a dozen people uselessly dead. It's not worth it." He touched his hat, flicked the horse with the whip, and drove off.

Anna watched him go and then turned back to the house. That picture—the man digging under the cottonwoods, Dr. Pendexter's buggy pulling out slowly toward town—had become fixed with familiarity. She walked through the living-room, untidy now and smelling of stale smoke from the night-long vigil of the menfolks, and went into her bedroom. When the sound of shuffling feet on the stairway came to her, along with the muffled talk and faint grunts of exertion, she closed the door. They were bringing Yace down in his coffin. She changed to her riding-clothes, Levi's and denim jumper, and went outside.

Her father and Jeff and Murray Seth had loaded the pine box into the spring wagon. Murray drove off, while Ben and Jeff came back to their horses. She mounted hers and the three of them rode out abreast. Ahead, she could see the crew, five men and the Chinese cook, strung out in a line, heading for the graveyard. She looked at her father and could see nothing in his face, no sorrow, no disgust, no pity, nothing but the bleak expression with which he faced the world nowadays. He had buried two sons, two brothers, and minor kinfolk, all with the same expression —or lack of it. His face was still swollen from the beating in the sheriff's office, as was Jeff's, but where Jeff's was cut and bruised, her father's was only puffed grotesquely. She looked away from them in loathing.

The services for Yace Bolling, shot the night the Bollings made their try for Buck Shields, were short, recited in an emotionless voice by Ben Bolling, his father.

Afterward, the little group broke up, and Anna started back with her father and brother.

"We better move Murray into Yace's room today," Ben said suddenly, and added by way of explanation, "Better protection for the house."

Anna grimaced in disgust. Her father never thought, except in terms of fighting men available, and how best to use them.

"You'll do nothing of the kind," she said coldly. "The help have their quarters. Are you going to turn your own house into a stables?"

"Stables?" Jeff asked, bridling.

Anna said contemptuously, "I'd much prefer a horse to Murray Seth."

"We need him there," Ben said with finality.

"Why?"

"I just told you. There's always been one of us at each corner of the house. In case they raid, there won't be a blind spot."

"How can they raid with Hagen Shields in jail?" Anna asked contemptuously.

A second later, she could have bitten her tongue out. Her father swung on her and said sharply, "Jail?"

"I—I thought they put him in jail for shooting Yace?"

Jeff pulled in from the other side of her and grabbed her horse's bridle, pulling him up. "You know something," Jeff said in a low voice. "Did Doc Pendexter say Hagen Shields was in jail?"

Anna said as forcibly as she could, "No. I thought you told me he was arrested."

Jeff's mouth lifted in a sneer. "You're lying." He looked across at his father.

"I think," Ben said slowly, "you're lying, Anna. Doctor Pendexter brought that news, because there's never been a hint of it before. What did he say?"

"Nothing, I tell you!"

"What did he say?" Ben insisted, his voice getting ugly. Jeff grabbed her by the wrist in a grip of iron.

"I'll cuff it out of you, sis," he promised. "What did he say?"

Anna struggled furiously. Jeff held to her wrist, and when she looked to her father for help, his face held no sympathy. Years ago he would have thrashed Jeff within an inch of his life for laying a hand on her, but now he was siding with Jeff.

Anna ceased struggling now, a wave of weary hopelessness washing over her. What was the use of fighting, of bucking fate? She said tonelessly, "Yes, he's in jail. And I don't know why."

Jeff dropped her hand and touched spurs to his pony. Ben followed, leaving her to ride home alone. She had done it now. It had been unwittingly said, but the result was the same. They would raid the Bridle Bit tonight, and in the morning more men would be dead.

When she arrived at the house, there was a fever of activity. The men were congregated at the bunkhouse, listening to Murray Seth. Her father was in the front room at the gunrack, and she could hear the clink of cartridges as he filled the belts.

She went up to him and said, "What are you going to do, Dad?"

"I think you know," Ben said, without looking at her.

"You can't! You just can't do it! Don't you realize that Lucy Shields will be there?"

"We'll let her go."

"And Pate, that boy?"

Her father looked up at her, his eyes wicked. "That boy shot Yace, Anna."

"To protect his brother. Oh, Dad, you can't do it! It's rotten and cruel and cowardly!"

Ben said coldly, "You just came back from the graveyard, Anna. Did you count the graves? Every one of them, with the exception of your mother's, was put there by a Shields. Now get out of the way. Go to your room."

Anna did. Outside, the men were changing horses. A couple of the hands were out in the pasture rounding up the horses and turning them into the corral. She knew how these men felt, and didn't wholly blame them for it. Hagen Shields, a month ago, had set fire to a line camp up in the mountains. Four Three B riders had been in that line camp, and Hagen Shields, from behind a tree, had shot each of them as they raced out of the blazing cabin. They found them there, face down, where he had left them, not even bothering to cover the bodies. These men feared and hated the kind of cautious murder that Hagen Shields planned. He had the patience of an Indian, taking advantage of every mistake, every lack of watchfulness in his opponent, until his very existence began to prey on their minds. But with him in jail, they would pay him back in kind tonight, and it made Anna sick to think about it.

An hour before dark, they rode out of the place, leaving only a skeleton crew to protect it. She had seen Murray Seth earlier ride over to the Dennises' to the north. The four Dennis riders added to the seven Three B men would outnumber the Shieldses, and they would have their way with them.

The triangle clanged in the dusk, the supper call to the remainder of the crew. Anna went out into the kitchen. Nobody would eat at the house tonight, for Jeff and her father and Seth were gone. Suddenly, she paused in the dusk of the kitchen. Now, while the men were at supper, was the time to act if she was ever going to. She slipped on a man's coat, got her flat-brimmed Stetson, and left the house.

At the corral there was just enough light to see that there was one horse left in the corral. Anna, hoping it was Streak, her bay filly, whistled softly. There was a short whicker in answer, and a horse walked over to the gate. Anna went inside the wagon shed, pulled her saddle from the poles, and saddled up, her hands trembling with excitement. She was going to do something that would have terrible consequences for her, perhaps, but she believed she could stand that. She could stand anything, now. Nothing that could happen to her would make things much worse.

Taking her pony by the reins, she led him through the gate. She was just closing it when a rider appeared from around the shed and pulled up at sight of her.

It was Murray Seth. She could tell his big-boned grace in the saddle and the high build of his gelding, and her heart sank within her.

Murray dismounted and led his horse over to her. "Oh, it's you," he said. "Where you going?"

"I'm afraid," Anna said quietly. "I'm going to town."

Seth laughed. "Afraid of what?"

"If we can raid them, they can raid us. I don't want to be here."

Seth came closer, and Anna, although she couldn't see his face, knew he was smiling crookedly, pleased with himself. The rank smell of horses, the smell of a dirty hostler, was about him, and it gagged Anna. She stepped backward, and was brought up against the corral poles.

"You have a pretty tough time of it here, don't you, Anna?" Murray began, his voice smooth with false sympathy.

"Have I ever told you I have?"

"No, but a man sees it. Jeff and Ben don't think of anything but fight. They've got no time for you, and you're lonesome, aren't you?"

"Will you get away from me?"

"Not yet," Murray said. "I come back here so I'd have a chance to talk to you alone. I've been waiting for this a long time."

"You've had your talk," Anna said. "Now get out of the way and let me ride out of here."

Murray took another step toward her, penning her tight against the corral. "Just a minute more," Murray said quietly. "I've been thinking about us, Anna. We're the only two people at the Three B who don't give a damn about this fight, and we're the only two that will come through it alive, you and me. And you'll need a man to run it, a husband. I'd treat you good, better than Jeff or Ben do. When it happens, will you remember that?"

Anna was so amazed that she could not answer. Murray Seth was already planning on the death of her father and Jeff, and of his position here afterward.

Murray, misunderstanding her silence, laughed comfortably and put his hands on her. The very touch of them seemed to unloose something in Anna. She struck out with her quirt and caught Murray across the face.

He stepped back, crying out in pain, and then he began to curse. Anna had lost all reason then. She went at him, lashing out with her quirt, crying with rage. Murray backed up, threw his arms in front of his face, and when that seemed to do no good, he took to his heels and ran behind the shed.

Anna stopped sobbing, and then turned and ran to her horse. Stepping into the saddle, she put the horse into a long lope across the park toward the town road. She was crying now out of hysteria and anger and disgust.

Murray Seth, gingerly touching the welts on his face, could hear her sobbing, and wondered what had got into her. He had spoken at the wrong time, had interrupted something. But what was it? Anna Bolling hadn't ridden to town at night before, never. And why was she riding tonight? Standing there, Murray Seth experienced the first jealousy he had ever felt in his life. To him, a pretty woman riding at night could mean only one thing, that she was riding to meet a man.

Murray Seth forgot his appointment at the Bridle Bit. He mounted and set out after Anna.

Tip was sitting at the roll-top desk, leafing through the reward dodgers that were deposited in the bottom drawer when he heard the door open. He turned to confront Lynn Mayfell and a girl whom he immediately recognized as Anna Bolling. The expression in the Bolling girl's face made him come to his feet quickly.

"What is it?"

"They're raiding the Shieldses' tonight," Anna said breathlessly. "I came as soon as I could."

Tip didn't wait for more. He pushed the two girls out, instructed Anna Bolling to wait for him at the hotel, directed a brief glance at the second-story window to see if the lantern in Hagen's cell block was still alight, and untied the reins of his horse at the tie rail in front of the sheriff's office. Down at the feed stable, he picked up Sheriff Ball, who was settling a feed bill, and together they headed out of town at a long lope. Caution told Tip to pick up more men, but he knew the time wasted in finding the men favorable to the Shieldses might prove too costly.

"They damn well didn't waste much time after Hagen got jailed," Ball said bitterly.

The ride seemed unending. But when they came to the bottleneck, passed through it, and rounded the bend, Tip pulled up. Far to the southeast, the night sky was lighted.

"They've burned the buildings," Ball said grimly.

Cutting across the park, Tip put his chestnut to a gallop. Not until this moment was the Vermilion county feud a brutal reality, and now he tried not to think of Lucy Shields, who might be trapped in that fire.

When they came in sight of the ranch, Tip breathed a sigh of relief. The barn behind the house was afire, its skeleton of logs still standing as it held between its ribs a great pillar of fire that crawled high into the sky and was capped by lazily turning banners of thick smoke. A racket of rifle fire, faint at this distance, was the only sound in the night.

Tip sized up the situation and said, "They're forted up behind those sheds, waitin' for the try at the house."

"We better hurry," Ball said.

Tip put out a hand. "We can't save the barn, and they'll hold the house long enough." He turned to Ball. "I'm going to make those Bollings sorry they ever put foot on this land. Come along."

Tip headed away from the fire toward the timber. Objects within a quarter of a mile of the fire were standing in faint relief. Achieving the timber, Tip said, "Spread out and work along the edge of the timber. When you find their horses, whistle."

Ball gave him a quizzical glance, then pulled off into the timber. Tip entered the timber about twenty yards, then, keeping parallel to the edge, he worked his way toward the fire. He had the feeling that he was losing precious time, that he should be doing something, but common sense told him there was no hurry, that the Shieldses could hold them off half the night.

Closer to the house now, he looked through the trees and saw the situation. Stretched in loose semicircle, from the wagon shed to the farthest corral, the Bolling men were behind shelter, pouring their fire into the house. Tip counted ten rifles. Along the narrow length of the house, on the barn side, four guns were returning the fire. Tip knew that the Bollings would have to wait now until the light from the fire was diminished enough to let darkness give them some protection. After that, the finish would be certain.

Ball's low whistle yanked him alert. He pushed back into the timber, and getting Ball's whistle again, he made for it. In a deep little gut over a low hogback, Ball was waiting for him. He could hear the uneasy movement of several horses.

"Ten of them," Ball said.

"Got a knife?"

"Yes. Why?"

"Lead 'em off, one by one. When they're clear, cut the cinch and bridle and give the pony a cut over the rump. These Bollings will walk home from this party."

He and Ball set to work. In a few minutes, all the Bolling horses had been driven off through the timber, the only reminder of their presence being a pile of useless saddles and bridles.

Afterward, their jobs understood, he and Ball parted.

Tip rode toward the fire. At the edge of the timber, he offsaddled, threw his saddle and bridle in the brush, took his rifle from the saddle boot, and made his way to the edge of timber. His chestnut started to follow him, but Tip drove him back into the timber. Finding a spot behind a log that commanded a good view of the house, he sat down, levered a shell into his Winchester, and waited. The fire was at its peak now, and the solid logs of the barn were caught well. The yard was light as day, and Bolling's men, keeping shelter between themselves and the house, were moving around hunting better positions.

When Ball's rifle opened up from a hundred yards above, Tip went to work.

He started with the wagon shed, throwing five shots into the deep shadow behind it. A man raced for the shelter of the corral, and Tip laid his last shot at him. The man seemed to trip. He lost his balance, dived on his face, skidded to a stop, and was still.

While Tip reloaded, he felt the calm settle on this scene now. Bolling's men were caught between two fires, afraid to shoot for fear their gun flashes would give them away. Doubtless, they were waiting to find the number of their assailants.

Tip slipped back into the brush, moved over twenty yards, and started in again. There were only four or five spots where the shadows could hide a man, and the corral was next in line. His first shot scattered four men, who ran for the shelter of the big corral. Ball's rifle, from a new location, harried them. When Ball's gun was empty, Tip took up the refrain, searching out each shadow.

Now a man broke loose and ran back into the night. Ball knocked him over, and swung back to the shadow of the blacksmith shop. His first shot there seemed to flush out men like a covey of quail.

Realizing now that it was impossible to find shelter here, where the fire set by their own hand was lighting their way to certain death, a kind of panic set in. Their only safety lay in achieving the darkness, and to do it they would expose themselves to the cross fire from timber and house.

Jeff Bolling was the first man to try. Tip was loading his rifle, and when he heard Ball's flat, hammering shots he looked up. Jeff was running, dodging, weaving, his pace unbroken, heading for darkness. At Ball's fifth shot, Jeff was swallowed up by the darkness. Now two others tried it, and Tip harried them, aided by the shots from the house. One of the men went down, but the other reached darkness. And now the others, Ben Bolling leading, made their dash. Tip's rifle was empty, and he cursed futilely as he fumbled in his hurry to reload. All but one of those five men made the darkness. That man went down, and started dragging himself toward the others. Ben Bolling paused long enough to give the man a hand. Tip, with Bolling at last between his sights, saw him stop, and he pulled off his mark. It was the only act of generosity he had seen a Bolling do, and even the thought of Buck Shields, drunk and helpless in that saloon with Ben Bolling pumping lead at him, could not make Tip pull the trigger. He let him go, and now the night was quiet.

Tip backed into the brush, whistled his chestnut to him and saddled up. Then he crashed through the brush, shooting now and then. Swinging in a wide loop, he could hear Ball doing the same thing. Leaving the timber, he headed for the spot where the Bolling crew had disappeared. Far over to the right, he heard the pounding of running feet. Way back in the timber, there was a sustained wild cursing which ended on the heel of a shot. Back there, Ball was crashing brush, shooting, feeding the panic these harried, unmounted men were feeling. Tip swung into the timber again to take up the refrain. Back and forth they rode, making the night wild with their yells and their shots and the noise. Afterward, when he pulled up to blow his pony, he saw Ball leave the timber and head toward the house. Tip swung in toward him.

Ball said grimly, "I don't think those murderin' sons will be back. I chased Ben Bolling until he dropped, and then rode him down, shooting wide of him. He was too scared to yell."

Tip said, "Let's see if anybody's hurt."

As they rode into the yard, Buck Shields let out a long yell and ran out of the house. Pate, lugging a rifle that was too big for him, crawled out the window. Cam Shields, his narrow face flushed with excitement, paused in the door and spat contemptuously. In the house, a lamp came alight.

Buck and Ball and Tip found one downed man behind the wagon shed. He was dead, shot in the head. The second man behind the blacksmith shop was dead, too. Buck said one man was a Three B rider, the other one of the Dennis boys. The third man, downed next to the wagon shed, was gone, taken by his friends, and the other wounded man, helped by Ben Bolling, trailed blood as far as the timber.

Back in the house, Lucy Shields was waiting for them. Tip, who had not seen her before, showed no sign of recognition as he was introduced, and Lucy, her eyes friendly, pretended this was their first meeting.

The house was a wreck. The windows were out, and the searching slugs of the raiders had broken everything breakable, chewing ragged holes in the log walls.

Buck looked around and then returned his glance to Tip. "That was close."

Cam Shields, still in the doorway, said meagerly, "And whose fault was that?"

Buck looked warningly at Tip and then turned to Cam, "You're a sorry *hombre*, Cam," he said quietly, without rancor. "Maybe you'd rather fry in a burnin' house?"

"I'd rather fight beside my own people," Cam said sparely, eyeing Tip. "I don't thank a man for jailin' our kin, then ridin' hell-for-leather to make up for the mistake."

On the heel of his words, Buck strode over to him, facing him. "You crawlin', yellow-bellied Indian," Buck said quietly. "Half an hour ago, Lucy had to load your gun for you, you were so scared."

Cam straightened up. "You're a damn liar."

Buck hit him then. He knocked him out into the hard-packed yard and strode out after him. Cam pushed himself up on his elbow and looked wickedly up at Buck, surprise and hatred and fear in his face.

"I'm roddin' this outfit now, Cam," Buck said meagerly. "Keep a civil tongue in your head, or I'll cut it out for you."

He looked up at Ball and Tip, who had stepped out now. "I apologize for him," he said. "He won't say that again."

Afterward Lucy and Buck went out with them to their horses. Tip dropped behind and walked with Lucy.

She said to him in a low voice, "I'm glad about Hagen. Buck told me about it."

Tip said, "I'd be a dead man except for your warnin'."

Lucy looked shyly at him, and then laughed shortly. "I guess we're square, then. No, we're not. Because you saved four of us tonight, I think."

Tip smiled faintly, and shook his head. "I'm afraid there'll be more nights like this. Maybe we won't be so lucky again."

"Lucky?"

"Anna Bolling warned me of this raid," Tip said slowly. "Otherwise I don't reckon we'd have known about it till it was over." He looked obliquely at Lucy. "You tell Buck that, will you? Only Buck."

Lucy nodded. As she approached the horses, she said softly, "Thank you. I won't forget this. None of us, Pate or Buck, either." When Tip looked at her there were tears in her eyes, and her lips trembled.

Looking at these Shieldses as he mounted his horse—Lucy, strong and quiet and capable; Buck, hard and responsible and generous; and Pate, shy and quiet, with judgment of these new friends suspended—Tip had the feeling that the Shieldses were in for a different life. If only this feud didn't engulf them before running its course.

Ball, silent up till now, expressed that thought on the

ride back to town. "Somethin's come over Buck. Lucy, too.
I like 'em, all but that cousin, Cam."

Tip agreed, feeling a weariness now. This fight tonight
would bring repercussions that he couldn't anticipate, and
neither could Ball. It would look, of course, as if they had
thrown in with the Shieldses, despite the fact that Hagen
Shields, the backbone of that family, was now in jail. The
Bollings wouldn't take it lying down, and neither would
Hagen Shields, or Cam.

The town was quiet when they rode in and left their
horses at the stable. They stopped at the Mountain saloon
for a drink, and parted there, Ball heading for the office
for a last look at Hagen Shields.

Tip went upstairs and knocked on Uncle Dave's door.
It was opened by Anna Bolling. Her face was tense, and
Tip could see that she had been crying.

"It's all right," Tip told her, and added shrewdly,
"Buck's all right, too. One of the Three B crew and one
of the Dennis crew were killed."

Anna murmured, "Thank God." She went over to the
chair and sat down by Uncle Dave. Tip waved carelessly
to him and said, "Evening, old-timer."

The old man smiled, and Tip took the other chair. He
was slack with weariness, and yet there were things he
wanted to ask Anna Bolling. But now was not the time,
he could see.

He said gently, "What will your dad and your brother
do if they find out you came to me?"

Anna said dispiritedly, "I don't know. I don't even
care."

"Will they find out?"

Anna was about to answer when she heard a clatter on
the stairs. Tip was standing up, his hand on his gun, when
the door opened.

Ball burst into the room, stopped, and said to Tip,
"Hagen Shields has been murdered in his cell!"

CHAPTER

7

IT WAS AFTER HAGEN SHIELDS'S FUNERAL the next morning. Buck was the only Shields there, for the Bridle Bit couldn't be left unprotected. Lynn Mayfell, Ball, Tip, the undertaker, who in everyday life ran the hardware store, and a handful of the professionally curious were the only ones attending the services in the small graveyard below town.

Afterward, Lynn came over to Buck. "Anna wants to see you," she said, and added to Tip, "You and the sheriff, too." She looked at Buck again. "You must have guessed that she thinks you might believe she was the decoy to get Tip away from the office."

Buck said simply, "I hadn't thought of it. I don't think much of it, either."

They walked back to the business section, Tip by Lynn's side. He was silent and moody today, and Lynn could guess what the trouble was. Tip figured he had blundered unforgivably in leaving Hagen Shields alone, although it was tacitly agreed that Hagen Shields's death removed the most stubborn obstacle in the settling of the Vermilion county feud. Tip's eyes were dark and sultry, and he didn't talk. When they reached the business part of town, mingling with the people, Tip had a belligerent look on his face, as if he were watching for the first sneer. And Lynn knew that people were sneering, people who had carefully avoided any part of the fight, except to criticize. In his present mood, Tip was reckless, and when they reached the hotel without trouble Lynn breathed a sigh of relief.

Tip, crossing the lobby behind Lynn, pulled up short, and regarded a drunk sleeping off his liquor in a lobby chair.

"That's what I need," Tip murmured, and turned into the saloon, leaving Lynn watching him. He went up to the bar, ordered a whisky, and downed a drink of it. It tasted like paint. He set the glass down in disgust. Nothing would ever taste right again until he'd made up for that blunder. And he couldn't bring Hagen Shields back to life.

He paid for the liquor and tramped upstairs, his mood ugly. He was making a mess of his job here, and he was no closer to discovering Blackie's murderer than he had been when he came. His eyes glinted stonily as he knocked on the door and went inside Uncle Dave's room. He interrupted a three-cornered conversation.

Ball was saying to Anna, "Nobody thinks you were sent, Anna, least of all Buck. It was just hard luck all around."

Buck said shyly, "You ain't goin' back there, are you, Anna?"

Lynn said quickly, "She's going to stay with me. We're getting rooms over the *Inquirer*."

Tip leaned against the wall until Buck, his eyes lingering on Anna, took his hat, said good-by, and went out. Lynn and Anna went out afterward, and Ball and Tip soon departed, heading for the sheriff's office.

Ball, by now, was as glum as Tip. At the office he took his hat off, slammed it on the desk, and sank into a chair. Tip watched him, his eyes sultry.

"What now?" he asked.

"Find out who cut down on Hagen," Ball said gloomily.

"Where you goin' to look?"

Ball said irritably, "How the hell should I know? Someone at the Three B did it. But I can't move till I know who. And I've tried that business before."

Tip said sharply, "Sheriff, you know damn well who killed Shields. One of the Three B outfit. But if you wait until you pin it on a certain one of them, you'll be gray-haired."

"What do you want me to do?" Ball asked.

"Let me do it," Tip said quietly. His eyes were ugly now,

and Ball caught some kind of a warning in them. "Me, I don't care who did it. They figure we'll be slowed down by no evidence, by fear that we'll hang it on the wrong man." He looked steadily at Ball. "Let's hang it on the wrong man, then. Hell, if the man we get didn't kill Hagen Shields, the chances are he's killed the marshal or dry-gulched a Shields."

"We can't do that!"

"Why not?"

"It ain't legal. We got to have evidence."

Tip shook his head. "Let a trial bring that out, Ball. Let's smash 'em. Let's fight first, and find out the truth afterward."

Ball was about to speak and didn't. He stared speculatively at Tip, and chewed the end of his mustache. Then he sighed. "It's nice to talk about. But they'll fight like hell before they'll let us take one of 'em!"

"Let 'em fight," Tip said angrily. "Damn but I'm tired of havin' to hide behind what's legal!" He walked over to Ball and confronted him. "Last night, after we cut those saddle cinches and chased them gunmen off the Bridle Bit, do you know what we should have done?"

"No," Ball said blankly.

"We should have rode up to the Three B and burned it to the ground!"

"But it isn't legal."

"That's the trouble!" Tip raged. "Nothing they do is legal! But when we take a crack at them, it's got to be!" He reached in his pocket and drew out his badge. "Me, I got a bellyful of it. Here's your badge! I'm goin' out and get somethin' done!"

Ball came to his feet. "Now, wait a minute," he said placatingly. "What do you aim to do?"

"If you'll lock him up, I'll go up there and pull Ben Bolling out of there and throw him in jail as Hagen's killer."

"But, dammit, Tip, he wasn't! We saw him at the Bridle Bit!"

Tip grinned wolfishly. "You think he'll admit that? If he does, I'll haul him in on that charge."

Ball shook his head dubiously.

"All I want to know," Tip went on implacably, "is whether or not I keep this badge and you lock up Ben Bolling."

"But you can't do it. They'll kill you."

"That's my lookout. What about it?"

Ball sank into the chair. "Well, I can't stop you. Sure, I'll lock Ben up. Lord knows, even if he didn't kill Hagen he's done enough else to hold him for."

"That's all I wanted to know," Tip said and headed for the door.

Tip was at the feed stable saddling up when Lynn came in.

"The sheriff told me what you're going to do," Lynn said. "It's insane, Tip!"

Tip straightened up slowly and rubbed the palms of his hands on his Levi's. "Who said it wasn't?"

"But you can't hope to get away with it, especially after last night."

"I'll get away with it."

Lynn stamped her foot in exasperation. "Tip, are you going to let that temper of yours kill you? It's kept you in trouble ever since you got here."

Tip said patiently, "Sure. I've been hearin' that from you since the night I got in town. That night you wanted me to run. Then you didn't want me to put in that reward notice." His voice got a little harder. "Well, I'm still alive."

"You're lucky."

"Not lucky. I won't be kicked around, that's all."

His face was set in a stubborn way that told Lynn she might as well try to move a mountain as change him. She stepped aside and watched him saddle a second horse and then mount.

"Good luck," she murmured, as he picked up the reins of the horse he was leading.

Tip rode out of town at a slow pace. He had lots of

time, and he wanted it to be dark when he arrived at the Three B. He felt angry with Ball and angry with Lynn, but most of all, he was angry and disgusted with himself. He had muffed his chance with Hagen Shields, had failed to hold him, try him, convict him, and use him as an example of what the other feudists of Vermilion could expect. He had been tricked and not very skillfully, and this time he was resolved he would not be tricked again. Hagen Shields's killer last night had climbed up on the roof, passed a rope around one of the two-by-fours that braced the false front, slipped down the rope to the window, and, dangling by one hand, shot Hagen Shields. If anyone saw him, he had not yet come forward. That was another thing that graveled Tip. How could a man hang there in the light of the lantern above the main street of a busy town and not be seen? He was seen, of course, but whoever saw him was cowed enough to keep silent. Tip cursed softly to himself. After he got through with the Bollings and the Shieldses and found Blackie's killer, he'd show this town something, too. Thinking that, his mind went back to Blackie's killer. The thought was nagging, insistent, on his mind most of the time.

It was not a pleasant ride for Tip. When he arrived, just at dark, on the edge of the park that held the Three B, a combination of self-accusation, anger, and disgust had pushed his temper to the point of recklessness. Here he was with two horses, one for Ben Bolling, one for himself. And over there was Ben Bolling. All he had to do was get Ben on the spare horse and herd him to town.

Tip waited until dark, and then set across the park. The supper triangle clanged, the noise of it riding faintly across the night to him. Tip increased his pace, swinging in a circle that would bring him in by the corrals. He walked his horses, and they were soundless on the thick grass of the park floor.

There was a light in the joined cookshack and bunkhouse, Tip saw, as he approached. Achieving the cover of the corrals, he moved along them, along the barn, and up to the corner of the wagon shed, which was the closest building to the bunkhouse, perhaps seventy yards away. Leaving the horses there, he skirted the bunkhouse again, walking toward the house. It was dark, and after watching it awhile, he decided that it was empty, so he would be safe enough from that direction. Going back past his horse to the pole corral, he could see there were a dozen horses there. Two gates, one from the pasture and one from the yard, opened into the corral. Tip scouted about the buildings until he found a roll of wire in the blacksmith shop. This he took and wired each corral gate solidly in three places. It would not stop pursuit, but it would delay it some.

Then, making sure his gun was loaded, he started toward the cookshack. Pausing short of it, he looked in the window. A long table ran the length of the room, with an overhead kerosene lamp above. Ben Bolling sat at the head of the table, Jeff Bolling to his right. Murray Seth sat beside Jeff. Tip couldn't count the others. A Chinese cook in shirt sleeves circulated with the food.

Tip glanced at the kitchen door, saw it was open, and made for it. He stepped inside, lifted his gun, and walked past the table to the dining-room door. For a moment, nobody saw him. He walked into the room, putting his back to the wall, and said above the murmur of voices, "Ben Bolling, stand up!"

The talk died. Jeff Bolling tried to rise out of his seat and couldn't because the bench held him. Ben Bolling dropped his fork, and slowly his hands settled to the table and started to slide under.

Tip said, "Keep your hands on the table," and edged his way along the wall. The eyes of seven men, wary and waiting for the chance they knew might come, followed Tip's course along the wall. Tip kept his eyes on Jeff and Ben Bolling and Murray Seth, figuring they would begin the play if it started.

Then Tip whipped out, "I said stand up, Bolling!"

Jeff Bolling's face was ugly, his eyes hot. He said,

"Damn, you won't get away with this, Woodring!"

Ben Bolling still sat. Tip took a step forward, put his foot on Bolling's chair, and shoved. It went over sideways, dumping Ben Bolling on the floor.

"I said stand up!"

Jeff and Murray Seth rose at the same time, and Tip swiveled his gun to them.

"Sit down!"

They sank down on the bench again. They were cocked, waiting for a chance to go for their guns.

Bolling came to his feet. Tip had already seen that he was minus belt and gun. Bolling said furiously, "What do you want of me?"

"You're under arrest for the murder of Hagen Shields," Tip said. "You're comin' with me to town."

"That's a lie!" Bolling said, his voice choked with anger.

"Prove it to a jury," Tip said. "Now back up toward that door."

The cook, down the room, made a sudden dash for the kitchen. Tip snapped a shot at him, and he stopped dead in his tracks and turned to face Tip, his face a sick green. Jeff and Murray Seth leaped away from the table, tipping the bench over backward. The other two hands behind Murray came to their feet.

The silence was as thin as wire as Tip taunted, "Four shells left. Anybody want to make a try?"

Nobody answered, and Tip circled toward the door until he was in back of Ben Bolling. "Now back up!"

Jeff Bolling waited patiently, and Tip knew what for. In the back of his own mind, a small glimmer of doubt was born. He felt himself sweating. Was he going to make it? Every man in this room, once Tip had stepped out that door, would pile out after him. Four slugs wouldn't stop them, and his horses were seventy yards away.

Tip rammed his gun in Bolling's back and said to Jeff, "Anybody you see moving out there might be Ben. And if you kill him, I'll come back and get you."

Grabbing Ben's collar, Tip hauled him back into the doorway, then, shoving him out into the yard, he raised his gun, shot out the light, and dodged out, just as a wild yell broke from Jeff. "Take the kitchen door!"

Tip swung on Ben, who was just coming up off his knees. He rammed his gun in Bolling's back and said, "Make for the wagon shed—and run!"

Bolling ran. Shots poured out of the cookshack door, and Tip could hear men running. The kitchen door crashed open, and more men poured out, all heading for the corral.

Tip realized now that he had been a fool to leave his horses in the path of these men, but it was too late to change it now. And he knew with certain conviction that he couldn't make his getaway riding through them.

Arrived at the place where his horses were tied, Tip said swiftly, "Untie those reins."

Bolling did, while Tip slipped his lariat off the horn. Then viciously he swung the coiled rope across the rump of his chestnut. The horse stampeded out into the night, and Tip cut the other horse across the rump. He went off in another direction.

A man yelled, "There they go!" and fired at the horses. Tip, his gun in Bolling's back again, said, "Get in the wagon shed!"

Bolling hesitated for a moment, then opened the door, the hot smell of dust and grease and leather drifting out. Bolling tripped over a wagon tongue, and Tip shoved him against the wall, ramming the gun in his midriff. "You make a move and I'll let this off."

"You wild damn fool!" Bolling whispered savagely. "You won't get away with it!"

Tip shoved the gun harder, and Bolling didn't speak. Tip could hear his labored breathing. Outside, men were yelling. Tip heard one pound past the shed, stop, and then yell wildly, "He's wired it."

"Try the other gate!" Jeff Bolling shouted. The light from a lantern showed under the door and then vanished.

Someone was cursing in a vicious, level monotone. Off by the cookshack, somebody was shooting.

Tip backed against the wall, his gun still in Bolling's side, and wondered if he would get away with it.

The crack under the door showed the lantern light again. Suddenly somebody wrenched the door open, and the lantern glow lighted up the shed. Tip had only the briefest glance at the interior, but he knew what had happened. A half-dozen saddles straddled a pole against the opposite wall, and these men had come for them.

Jeff Bolling, gun in one hand, preceded the man with the lantern into the shed. He heard Tip's movement, stopped short, wheeled, and saw Tip and Ben Bolling. Only now, Tip had Ben Bolling in front of him, the gun rammed in Bolling's back.

Jeff's eyes glinted like an animal's in that light. His gun was leveled at Ben.

"This is the payoff," he said thickly. "Step out from behind him."

"Back up," Tip countered. "Damn you, back out of here or I'll shoot!"

Tip shoved Ben a step ahead of him, and Jeff backed up. Tip went on, and Jeff backed clear of the door and out into the yard, his eyes wild with murder.

Tip put his back against the side of the shed, hauling Ben close in front of him. Four riders, motionless and staring at him, all with guns drawn, watched Jeff Bolling for a signal.

Tip said in an iron voice, "Pull a horse out of there and saddle him, you with that lantern. Put it down!"

He shot once at the man's feet. The man leaped aside, swinging up his gun, and Jeff raised a hand. "Give him one," Jeff said softly. The rider put down the lantern and backed into the corral gate. The horse was saddled and led out.

Jeff was watching, his gun leveled, and Tip listened intently for anyone approaching from around the corner of the wagon shed.

The rider led the horse over to Tip and then Tip said, his voice wicked with warning, "Back against the corral poles, the lot of you!"

"Hell with you!" Jeff Bolling cried. "Try to make it if you can!"

Tip shot again, and his slug whipped through Jeff's boot top and kicked dust against the lantern.

"I've got one shot left here, Bolling," Tip said wickedly. "I'll give you two seconds to move."

Jeff, cursing hysterically, backed away, and so did the others, until their backs were against the corral poles. This was going to break in a moment, Tip knew, and he would have to act fast.

He shoved Ben ahead of him, grabbed the reins of the horse, and turned him around. "Get up!" Tip ordered. "Leave that left stirrup free!"

The horse was between Tip and Jeff. Ben, cursing with rage, swung into the saddle. Tip put his left foot in the stirrup, grabbed the horn with his left hand, swung up, and with his free boot raked the horse's flank. The horse lunged forward with his double and lopsided burden, plunging for the corner of the woodshed. Tip snapped his last shot at the lantern, and saw it kick over and go out, just as Jeff yelled, "After him!"

They rounded the corner of the wagon shed. A man afoot, racing around the corner, was knocked spinning by the horse, and then they were in darkness.

Ben Bolling, who had counted Tip's shots, too, now swung his free arm at Tip. Tip lifted his gun, brought it down in across Bolling's head and shoved. Bolling slacked out of the saddle and fell. Tip heard him hit the ground with a grunt, then his thick voice rose in the cry, "Over here! Over here!"

Tip swung his right leg over the saddle now, just as the first shots from the wagon shed searched for him in the dark. He rounded the corner of the house now, crouched low over the horn, ramming fresh loads in his gun. Racing past the gallery, he flogged the horse with the reins, until

the pony stretched out in a terrified run. Tip slipped out
of the saddle then, hit the grass, fell, rolled, and came to a
stop against the corner of the porch.

He rose, stumbled, caught himself, and ran for the
shelter of the porch, flattening against the wall, just as
three riders boiled past him. He heard one man yell, "That
horse is windbroke! Ride him down!"

Tip hugged the wall, and five more riders cut around
the corner, and then there was a silence.

Tip peered around the corner, saw nothing, and then
ran back toward the wagon shed, his mind clouded with a
fury that did not let him know that his leg was hurting. It
was only when he fell and struggled up again that he knew
he was hurt, and then he didn't care. Ben Bolling, as he
had seen, was not among those six riders—and Ben Bolling
was under arrest.

He pounded around the corner of the wagon shed to
find the lantern guttering in the same spot. And Ben
Bolling, alone, was closing the corral gate. One whole side
of him was a smear of dust.

When he saw Tip he stopped, as if he were not going to
believe his eyes, and then his mouth opened with wordless
cursing. Tip grabbed him by his open vest and shook him,
and said wildly, "You're comin' with me, Bolling. Now
get two horses out here. If they come back before you're
through, I'll gun you, so help me, and shoot my way clear."

Bolling gave up then. He brought out two horses, put
bridles on them, and then, Tip, in an agony of waiting,
said, "Never mind the saddles. Get on."

He swung up after Bolling. He was waiting for his horse
to pitch, but Bolling was too beaten to have thought of
giving him a salty horse.

Tip cut Bolling's horse across the rump, and they angled
off toward the cookshack. The cook, standing in the doorway, saw them, dodged inside, and they pounded past him.
Seconds later, his rifle hammered futilely into the night.

Tip held to a gallop, hugging the flank of Bolling's
pony, until they made the timber. Then he pulled up and

CHAPTER
8

"WHERE'D YOU HEAR THAT?" Buck demanded of Pate at dinner next day.

"Clem Dockstader," Pate said, his eyes bugging. "It's all over town. He brung him in last night, they said. Ben Bolling looked like he'd been drug through a rifle barrel backward."

"And he's in jail now?" Buck asked.

When Pate nodded, Buck looked up at Lucy, who had stopped her serving long enough to listen to Pate's story.

"On what charge?" Lucy asked.

"Killin' Uncle Haig."

Cam Shields, already finished, tilted back in his chair and sucked on a toothpick, his eyes sleepy-looking and at the same time watchful. "He couldn't of killed Haig," Cam drawled. "He was right here when Haig was shot."

"What do you care?" Buck asked. "He's in jail, that's the main thing."

"No, it ain't the main thing," Cam said irritably. "If Ball can throw them Bollings in jail on a bogus charge, it's a leddy-mortal cinch he can throw us Shieldses in, too, if he notions it."

Buck put down his fork. "The Shieldses aren't doin' anything that they could be put in jail for, Cam. You better get that through your head."

Lucy put in, looking at Cam, "Ben Bolling tried to burn us out and kill us. Don't you think that's enough to jail him for?"

"I ain't talkin' about what Ben Bolling done," Cam said, his narrow face stubborn. "I'm talkin' about what he didn't do. And he never killed Haig."

"He done just as bad!" Pate said hotly. His mop of tow

listened, holding the bridle of Bolling's horse. Far off to the north, a racket of gunfire drifted to him.

He turned to Bolling and said mildly, "It'll be just twice as hard to break you out of where you're goin'. Now, get on."

hair lay in an unruly wing over his forehead, partially covering one eye. Cam reached over and mussed Pate's hair and grinned. "All right, younker. Don't take my hide off."

Pate didn't like to be treated like a ten-year-old, and he subsided in sullen silence. Buck assigned the work for the afternoon, then went out. Presently he rode into town. Pate went out to the corral to saddle up, and Cam followed him. The timbers of the barn were still smoldering. Cam's face was thoughtful as he leaned on the corral poles, watching Pate snake out a new horse for the afternoon riding. When, on the first cast, Pate laid a loop over his pony, Cam said, "You're better at that than I am, Pate."

Pate flushed with pleasure, knowing it was true. He was an all-around better hand than Cam was, only Buck had forbidden him to carry a gun of any sort, or even discuss the Bollings with anybody. Buck was an old woman in some ways, Pate thought, but he was a lot more of a man than Cam.

He threw his saddle on the gelding under Cam's watchful gaze.

"Did you see Ben Bolling, Pate?"

"Hunh-unh. Ball wouldn't let me in."

"Was he marked up, did you hear?"

Pate said idly, "I never heard."

"Of course, them lawmen would half kill Haig before they throwed him in jail, but not a Bolling. He's too high and mighty to touch."

Pate ceased work. "Come to think of it, they just said Ben was dirty, like he'd been wrassled around."

"Haig wasn't dirty," Cam said grimly, "he was bloody. He was a Shields, though, and there's a difference."

Pate looked at him. "You mean, they beat up Uncle Haig before they throwed him in jail, just because he was one of us?"

"That's what I mean," Cam said, a spurious bitterness in his voice. "That-there sheriff's office is fightin' for the Bollings, and doin' it legal, too."

"I don't see that," Pate said, his interest roused now.

"You don't see no Bollings dead, do you?" Cam challenged. "You don't see no buildings of theirs burned down."

"But Ben Bolling is in jail."

"He'll go free," Cam scoffed. "Why, they ain't even holdin' him on a charge that will hold water, and Tip Woodring knows it." He shook his head. "That's just a front. They're tryin' to make it look to Buck like they was goin' to be fair. Fair!" he snorted contemptuously.

"You think they won't hold Ben?"

"How can they? All Jeff Bolling or Murray Seth has got to do is swear Ben was with them, and he'll walk out of that jail. Haig went out of it a dead man."

Pate knew that was so, and he felt sudden anger. This morning, he had thought Tip Woodring a pretty fine *hombre,* but when Cam pointed out a few things it looked a little different. Ben Bolling wasn't hurt, and he'd been arrested on a charge that they'd have to free him on. Pate knew that because he'd seen Ben Bolling here the night of the fight. Uncle Haig was arrested and died in jail. Ben Bolling, a far more guilty man in Pate's eyes, would walk out of jail a free man.

Cam, watching Pate shrewdly, said, "That's what gravels a man, Pate. Here this old Ben Bolling has killed half our family and tried to burn us out. No worse man was ever met. Even his girl won't stay around him. He's a killer with a plumb black heart. And he's goin' free."

Pate said hotly, "Somebody ought to shoot him!"

"Sure they should," Cam agreed, adding, "They shot Haig in jail, didn't they?"

Pate suddenly thought of something, and looked swiftly at Cam. Cam wasn't looking at him; he was drawing circles in the dust with the toe of his boot. Pate was glad Cam hadn't seen him then, because Cam sometimes had a pretty good idea of what a man was thinking, without having to be told.

Pate turned back to his cinching, and Cam looked up.

"Look here, Pate," Cam said. "If Ben Bolling gets out of jail, the chances are he's goin' on the warpath again. And you ain't carryin' a gun."

"Buck said not to," Pate murmured sullenly.

"What would you do if you met some of them Bollings, or one of the Dennis outfit this afternoon?"

"Run, I reckon."

"And what if they run you down?"

Pate bit his lip. "Nothin'."

Cam lifted out his six-gun and offered it to Pate. "Here, you better carry this."

Pate looked at it longingly and then away. "No, Buck said not to."

"Buck ain't got good sense," Cam said. He let a little of his real contempt for Buck slip into his voice, and that was a mistake. Pate looked up sharply.

"Who said he ain't?"

"I never meant that, really," Cam said hurriedly. "I meant, he don't understand that you're in danger."

Pate said firmly, "If he thought I was in danger, he'd tell me to carry a gun. If you want me to carry one, you better ask Buck. He's the Big Augur around here now, Cam, not you."

The spell was broken now, and Cam could see he had lost. He watched Pate ride away, and his lip was curled in contempt. He almost had him there for a while, almost convinced him that Ben Bolling needed killing. Somehow, this gave Cam a feeling of power, and he smiled to himself. He saw where he'd made his mistake. If he'd approached it from another angle, like Pate would be doing Buck a favor and probably save his life if he did to Ben Bolling what the Bollings did to Hagen, then Pate would have been primed to kill. But, no, he'd muffed it.

He turned toward the house, walking slowly. He was a fool to try and bring any of his cousins in on this. They hadn't liked Hagen Shields, simply because Hagen was a better man than Buck. So they couldn't be expected to feel the way he did about Hagen's death. The idea that had come to him when he listened to Pate's news this noon was suddenly more than an idea. It was a resolve that had been sidetracked for a moment out there in the corral, but now it was back, hard and shining and implacable.

Lucy watched him go through the kitchen to his bedroom and return with a rifle. She said, "You aren't riding off the place, are you, Cam?"

"Oh, no," Cam said easily. "I saw some deer sign over across the *cienega* yesterday. I think I'll make a try for them." He went out.

Lynn Mayfell and Anna Bolling cooked their first supper in their new rooms above the *Inquirer*. Originally the rooms had been leased by two lawyers attracted to Hagen by reports of the feud and the possible lawsuits that would follow. But there were no lawsuits in this feud, and after the lawyers had got a bellyful of waiting for clients that never came in, they drifted away.

The supper dishes were stacked, and Lynn and Anna were working on curtains that would afford them some privacy this night. The big table in their front room was covered with material and they were sewing industriously, chatting, when they heard slow footsteps on the outside stairway. Lynn went to the door and found Tip Woodring climbing the stairs at a snail's pace. His leg was stiffened by bandages, for among all the wild shots thrown his way last night at the Three B, one had hit him in the thigh. It was a clean wound, but one that was painfully sore and stiff.

But whatever pity Lynn had felt for him had vanished this afternoon when he announced that he was making them a visit tonight, and that the reason for that visit was to question Anna Bolling about Blackie Mayfell. Lynn was all for waiting, saying that in her own good time Anna Bolling would tell her of discovering Blackie. Tip, goaded by impatience, had refused. The only way they'd learned what little they did know was by demanding it and getting it, wasn't it? This, of course, led to argument which grew

heated and ended in a quarrel. All Tip would promise
was that he wouldn't give Lynn's identity away. Lynn had
left him, her face flushed with anger, and wondering if she
were turning into a shrew. The number of times she had
talked to Tip Woodring without being infuriated by something he said or did could be counted on one hand. It
worked the other way, too. Her very presence seemed to
inspire Tip with a cross-grained deviltry. But Lynn didn't
care what he thought of her, as long as she knew her quar-
reling stemmed from the fact that she was trying to dis-
cover the murderer of her father.

Tip stepped inside and said, "Evenin'," to Anna and
nodded a little coolly to Lynn.

Tip said to Anna, "I'm sorry I had to do that to your
father, Anna."

"Don't be sorry, Tip. You had to do it. Sit down, please,"
Anna said. Tip hobbled over to a chair and settled into it,
putting his hat on the floor.

Lynn thought angrily, *He's mealy-mouthed. He knows
he's going to bully her, and starts it out by being polite.*

But as soon as Tip was seated, he said, "Anna, this is
going to be a tough night for you. I've got a hunch you'll
be sorry I came, mighty sorry."

Lynn didn't know why, but she felt relieved at that, and
rather proud of Tip, although she wouldn't admit it to
herself. "I'll go finish the dishes," she said.

"You'll do nothing of the sort," Tip said. "You'll stay
here. Anna will need your help. When I get too rough, you
can tell me to call off the dogs." He grinned in a friendly
way, and Anna, bewildered, looked at Lynn for help. Lynn
shrugged.

"What are you trying to tell me?" Anna said.

Tip looked at her troubled face. It was a strong face,
not beautiful, but there was character in it. She looked like
a girl who had met trouble face to face, and Tip felt
ashamed that he was going to make her face it again. He
pulled out his pipe, packed it, lighted it, and said, "It's
about Blackie Mayfell, Anna."

Something like terror passed fleetingly over Anna's face, and Tip felt a pity for her. He hardened himself, however, and went on. "Blackie Mayfell was killed on Three B land. We know that."

"Who is 'we'?" Anna asked shrewdly.

Tip flushed. That had been a slip of the tongue. "The man who sent me and myself."

"Who did send you?" Lynn asked curiously. She had been wanting to ask this a long time, and she was glad now that Anna had given her the chance.

Thoughtfully, Tip leaned forward, resting his elbows on his knees, and said to Anna, "I'll tell the truth if you will, Anna. How about it?"

"What are you going to ask?" Anna said, color creeping into her face.

Tip said sharply, "I'm supposed to be asking the questions, Anna, not answering them."

"Stop your bullying," Lynn said quietly.

Tip grinned swiftly and settled back in his chair. "I came here from Forks on a business proposition, Anna," he said. "I'm earnin' ten thousand dollars if I find Blackie's killer." He went on to tell of the deal with Rig Holman.

When he was finished, Anna said bluntly, "That's not much to your credit, Tip. Finding a man so you can blackmail him."

"I know it," Tip said quietly. "Only I got starved out down south. Ten thousand dollars means the difference between starvin' again and ownin' a nice spread. I don't care much about the rules for gettin' it, either, blackmail or no blackmail."

"That's been pretty obvious," Lynn said.

There was amusement in his eyes as he looked briefly at Lynn, and then back to Anna. "Well, I came clean, Anna. I need your help. Will you give it to me?"

"I don't think so," Anna said slowly.

Tip went on stubbornly. "We know you discovered Blackie Mayfell's body. We also know you didn't tell anybody, and that you let it be discovered later by Jeff or

Murray Seth or by your dad. They took him and dumped him on Bridle Bit range. Why?"

"Haven't you heard we're fighting?" Anna asked dryly.

"Why?" Tip asked again. "They didn't tell Ball that they'd seen any of the Shieldses murder Blackie, so they didn't even do it for a frame-up. Why did they do it?"

Anna was silent.

"Why, when you found Blackie's body at first, Anna, didn't you tell your family?"

Anna was silent, her mouth set in a firm line.

Tip said, "You're not going to tell me?"

"I'll tell you this much," Anna said hesitantly. "This man was dead when I came upon him. He'd been shot in the back."

"I know that," Tip said impatiently. "I want to know the rest of it. Who are you protecting? Why was Mayfell moved off your land, with no attempt to frame the Shieldses? Your brothers wanted to keep it quiet. You wanted to keep it quiet. I want to know why."

Lynn was looking at Anna in breathless suspense. When Anna looked at her, Lynn's gaze fell away, and she relaxed her hold on the edge of the table. She laughed shakily and said, "For heaven's sake, Anna, nobody thinks you killed this man. Why don't you tell Tip, so he'll leave you alone?"

"I can't," Anna said in a low voice. "I can't do it. You can do anything to me you want, but I won't tell!" She looked at Tip. "I won't!"

Tip looked helplessly from Anna to Lynn. "What's the matter with her?"

"Too much Tip Woodring," Lynn said dryly. "Leave her alone, Tip. Or are you going to put her in jail?"

Baffled, Tip came to his feet. Lynn had been right. Anna wasn't going to tell him, and the way it looked she wasn't going to tell Lynn, either. He picked up his Stetson and held it by the brim with both hands, looking searchingly at Anna.

"I'm trying to help you."

"Oh, I know you are, Tip. But I can't tell you. I would

if I could, but it's no use asking."

Tip said shortly, "Good night," and walked to the door. He was going to have to do it the hard way, and that would hurt Anna. He nodded to Lynn and hobbled slowly downstairs.

Ball was at the office, and when Tip went in he looked over his newspaper. "Well?"

"She won't talk."

"I thought so."

Tip said suddenly, "I'll make a bargain with you, Sheriff." When Ball became attentive, Tip said, "Ben Bolling knows something about this. They all do. I'm going to offer Bolling his freedom—*this time*—if he'll tell me what he knows about Blackie's murder." Ball looked noncommittal, and Tip continued. "I'll corral him again, because he'll make a try for us or the Shieldses again. In a week I'll have him back in jail. Besides, you said yourself we haven't got grounds for holdin' Bolling."

Ball said dryly, "Goin' back on what you said last night, eh?"

Tip flushed. "You're damn right I am. *I want to know about Blackie!*"

The sheriff folded his paper and sighed. "All right. Only you're a jughead, Tip. The whole U. S. Army couldn't take Bolling out of that camp again."

"You watch," Tip said. He hobbled up the stairs to the cell block, took down the lantern hanging in the corridor, and went over to Bolling's cell. Ben Bolling came to a sitting position at his approach. Tip set down the lantern on the floor, put his hands on the bars, and said, "Bolling, how'd you like to leave this place?"

"Come to your senses, have you?"

"Not any," Tip said. "I'll tell you something, Bolling. I know you didn't kill Hagen Shields, because I saw you there at the Bridle Bit. But if you give an alibi that will free you, you've got to admit you were there tryin' to burn Shields out. And if you give that alibi you're puttin' yourself open to arrest again. So you've kept your mouth shut, because if you opened it, you'd be in jail either way."

Bolling said nothing.

"We'll just forget about this whole business this time if you'll talk."

"About what?"

"What do you know about Blackie Mayfell? You discovered his body after Anna discovered it. You took it over on Shields range. But you didn't try to frame Buck or Hagen or Cam Shields with the murder. Why didn't you? Who are you protectin'?"

Bolling shook his head slowly. "That's the bargain, is it? You let me out for that information?"

"Yes."

"Go to hell." He lifted his feet off the floor, ready to lie down, just as a rifle hammered out from across the street. The bar next to Ben Bolling's head clanged, and the slug sirened off into the wall. Tip kicked the lantern over, whipping out his six-gun. From the corner of his eye he had caught the gun flash from the room of a building across the street. He emptied his gun in a staccato roar at the gun flame, then wheeled and plunged downstairs. His leg knifed pain, but he hit the office floor, staggered, caught himself, and ran out after Ball, who was standing on the sidewalk.

"Across the street!" Tip said. He ran past Ball, dodged under the hitchrail, fell, got up, and Ball passed him. They knifed in between two buildings and ran back to the alley. They got only the sound of a horse galloping down that blackness, and they both emptied their guns at the sound, knowing it was futile.

"Did he get Bolling?" Ball asked.

"No."

Ball breathed a relieved sigh. "Now, who could that be?" he murmured softly.

"Get the lantern," Tip said. "I'm goin' to have a look around here."

Tip didn't move until Ball returned with the lantern, then they set about looking for tracks. In the hard-packed cinders of the alley, nothing was plain. They saw where his horse had been ground-haltered, saw where he hit the ground after sliding off the roof. Tip said, "Give me a boost."

"I'll go up," Ball said. "You hand up the lantern."

Tip gave him a leg up and then handed up the lantern. Ball traveled the ridgepole to the false front, and paused once to call, "There's a little blood up here."

Tip grunted, and Ball went on. At the false front, over the top of which the bushwhacker could get a clean look into the second-story window of the jail, Ball found only a scattering of matches, indicating the man had been there a long time.

He came down, dropped heavily to the ground, and dusted off his hands. "He was forted up there waitin' for somebody to bring that lantern into the cell block, so he could see to sight."

Tip cursed under his breath, and led the way back between the buildings. Suddenly he stopped and kneeled, holding the lantern close. There lay a Winchester carbine, its stock broken at the grip.

Tip said, "We must have stepped on it." He picked up the stock and turned it over. There, on the other side, were burned the initials *C. S.*

"Cam Shields," Sheriff Ball murmured. "That fits right enough, don't it?"

Tip nodded, rising. "That's the best news we've had in a long stretch, Sheriff. Will the county commissioner let you have any money?"

"What for?"

"Why, put out a reward for Cam Shields and drive him out of the country. With him gone, we know what the Shieldses will do. They'll keep the peace. And it takes two to make a fight. Whenever the Bollings step out of line from now on, we'll nail them. The Shieldses," he added slowly, "are out of this feud, I reckon."

CHAPTER
9

WHEN CAM SHIELDS had achieved the end of the canyon and the lip of the rim, he pulled up, fighting down his panic in order to listen. For a long moment he sorted out the night sounds, but among them he could not hear the pounding of running horses. Slowly his heart stopped racing, and at the same time the throb in his left arm came into his consciousness. He put his hand there and it came away wet, and for a second he was dismayed. Then he ripped off his neckerchief, fashioned a bandage, and then gingerly raised his arm. The numbness was gone, and he could move it. He laughed softly. That wild devil of a Tip Woodring was lucky, but not that lucky.

He sobered instantly when he remembered the rifle he had dropped when he was hit. The slug had knocked him off balance, and he had dropped everything to grab for the ridgepole. After that, a wild and savage desire to get out of there came over him, but he knew that the rifle had slid off the roof to the ground. And no matter how much he repeated to himself that it didn't matter, that it wouldn't be found, he knew he was lying. Tip Woodring would find it, and on its stock read his initials. *C. S.*

Cam sat there in the dark, knowing without putting it into words that this was one of those turning-points in his life. The past was dead, and he couldn't go back to it. If he did, it would be to face jail and the desertion of Buck and Lucy and Pate. Of Tip Woodring, he could be dead certain. If Tip would haul Ben Bolling from under the nose of eight of his men and jail him, he would take Cam for attempting the same crime. No, he couldn't go back, because the bridges were burned.

He had two choices now. He could ride out of this country, leaving his cousins to make their peace with the Bollings, or he could stay. The latter course meant that from now on he would ride the dark trails, a fugitive, often hungry and cold, hunted by both sides and in constant danger. A wave of self-pity washed over him then, but a throb of excitement came, too. They couldn't catch him, and alone he could do more to the Bollings than Buck and Tip Woodring put together.

He classed Buck and Tip together now, and hated them both—Buck with his sniveling justice, Tip with his tough John Law pose. Ever since Cam came here, he'd had his own ideas about fighting this fight. They included bushwhack and murder and rustling and long rifle shots on lonely roads. Haig had kept him in line, and Buck was worse. Well, he didn't have them to answer to now. There were the Bollings, the same as they had always been. And there was Tip Woodring, too. He'd pay them off in his own way.

The first thing, of course, was to get some food. Could he get back to the Bridle Bit before Sheriff Ball reached it? He'd try.

When he reached the Bridle Bit, his horse was almost foundered. He left his pony at the corral, and made a cautious circle of the house. It was quiet. Lucy, in the front room, was sewing, and Pate was reading at the table. Cam went back to the corral, cut out a fresh horse, saddled him, and led him up to the house.

When he stepped in, Lucy looked up, and Cam closed the door behind him. "Where's Buck?" he asked.

"Looking for you," Lucy said. Then she caught sight of the bandage and came to her feet. "What happened to you, Cam?"

Cam smiled wolfishly. "Just a present from Tip Woodring, that's all." He tramped into his room. Lucy and Pate followed, standing in the doorway, silently watching him.

Cam ripped two blankets from his bed, took down a belt of forty-five shells, a belt of .30-30 shells, and stacked them all on the kitchen table.

"Where are you going, Cam?" Lucy asked presently.

Cam wheeled to snarl at her, "I'm clearing the hell out of here!"

"But why?"

"To keep from roosting in jail," Cam sneered. He went into Buck's room and came back with a rifle. "Tell Buck I'm taking this."

"He won't like that," Pate said gravely.

Cam said mockingly, "Oh, won't he, now? Well, suppose you tell him to try and get it back."

Lucy said calmly, "Cam, you've been up to something. What is it?"

"Ask Woodring," Cam jeered. He turned to survey the kitchen cupboards. "I want a sack of biscuits, a sack of coffee, a fry pan, two empty cans, and some matches. Make it quick!"

Lucy obediently did his bidding. Cam rolled all of it except the rifle in his bedroll, hacked Lucy's clothesline to pieces to tie it, then took rifle and bedroll and went out to his horse. Pate held the lantern in silence while he laced the bedroll behind his cantle. He had just finished when he turned his head to listen. He could hear a horse out there in the dark.

He wheeled, knocking the lamp out of Pate's hand, then bolted into the saddle and raced off into the dark.

In a moment Buck pulled up beside Lucy. "Wasn't that Cam?"

"Yes. He's in some kind of trouble."

Just then Cam's rifle cracked out. The window Lucy was standing beside jangled down onto the hard-packed dirt, and Lucy ran for cover. Buck sat his horse, cursing in a half-whisper.

Cam sheathed his gun, laughing, and urged his horse onward. That ought to give them some idea of what he thought of the whole hard-scrabble lot of them. He'd win their fight for them, and then wouldn't even bother to go back and get their thanks. That, too, would show his opinion of them.

He rode on into the timber, headed roughly east, remembering a camping-spot in a lonely canyon. He arrived there past midnight, staked out his horse, and, not bothering to build a fire, spread out his blankets and crawled into them. He smoked a couple of cigarettes, thinking, before he turned over to sleep. Suddenly he laughed aloud.

Jeff Bolling was in a wicked mood at breakfast. Yesterday afternoon, fired by a bottle of whisky, he had sworn that he was going in and pull Ben out of jail. He had drunkenly cursed his riders, dared them to go with him, until Murray Seth, the coolest head in the lot, had to hit him. He did a good job of it. Jeff, nerves on wire edge, had needed the fourteen hours of sleep he had got last night. This morning, with a clearer head, he remembered only vaguely the things Murray said he had done. It made him shiver to think what would have happened had he gone into Hagen, primed with whisky-guts to break his father out of jail. Still, Murray shouldn't have hit him. And the crew was still smarting under the taunting they had received. They were being pushed almost to the limit, Jeff knew, and it wouldn't be long before they decided to drift on. And Ben was still in jail.

Finished with breakfast, Jeff got some hot water from the cook and shaved and changed to a clean shirt. He felt better. Murray was waiting on the bunkhouse steps for orders as Jeff came up to him.

"I'm goin' into town," Jeff said.

Murray said nothing.

"There's nothin' they can arrest me for."

"Nobody said there was."

"All right. I'm goin' in and talk to Ball. He knows Dad didn't kill Shields." When a look of wariness crept into Murray's eyes, Jeff laughed jeeringly. "Dad won't tell, if that's what's worryin' you."

"Why should he?" Murray said indifferently. "I done him the biggest favor he's ever got."

"Yeah. Landed him in jail."

Murray's gaze whipped up to Jeff. "Maybe killin' a marshal and gettin' Hagen Shields out of the way ain't worth layin' a few days in jail for!"

"All right, all right," Jeff said pacifically. "Sure it is. Now get the horses. You're goin' in with me."

Murray rose and went over to the corral, cut out two horses and saddled them, and led them over to the bunkhouse. He and Jeff mounted and headed across the park. The wind off the Vermilions riffled the grass which was just beginning to cure now, and there was the tang of fall in the air. No roundup this year, Jeff was thinking; too many other things to think about.

They entered the timber, riding side by side, passed the ragged edge of it, and were then in the cold gloom of the pines. Jeff raised a hand to button his shirt collar when a voice ripped out of the brush, "Pull up!"

Jeff did, turning his head toward the sound of the voice. There, leaning against the trunk of a pine not ten yards off the side of the road was Cam Shields, and he had a six-gun in his hand.

Jeff knew Cam Shields only as Hagen Shields's son, but there was enough of Hagen in Cam's face to make Jeff shiver. His face turned a little green as he slowly raised his hands. This time the Shieldses had got the drop on him. Murray Seth whispered hoarsely, "I ain't a Bolling, Shields. Remember that."

Cam laughed. "I don't aim to cut down on you. I just want to talk."

"T-Talk?" Jeff stammered.

"Hell, I can't ride into your place without gettin' shot out of the saddle." He paused. "You and me, Bolling, have a lot of things to talk over. As soon as you shuck them guns and throw them on the other side of your pony, you can get down and we'll parley. You too, Seth—only you wait till Jeff's got rid of his guns before you throw yours."

Jeff wondered if this was simply a ruse to disarm him, then kill him. But whatever it was, he had no other choice. And he didn't intend to make a try for Cam, not with that gun leveled at him. He flipped his guns out into the road, and Murray did the same.

"Now get down and walk over here," Cam said.

They walked up the low bank, and Cam backed away and stopped, leaving about ten feet between them. Then he lowered his gun and squatted against the base of a pine and cuffed his Stetson back off his narrow forehead.

"Bolling, you and me have been fightin' here for a couple of years. We're still fightin'—only neither one of us is fightin' the right *hombre*."

Jeff stared at him, puzzled.

"One of us ain't goin' to lick the other," Cam went on. "We're goin' to get licked, right enough, both of us. Right down to the ground. *But it'll be Tip Woodring that done it!*"

"I thought he was helpin' you," Jeff said skeptically.

Cam touched the bandage on his arm. "Does that look like it?"

"Hell, I never loved him. What did he do to you?"

"Not only to me," Cam said bluntly, "to you, too. Last night he tried to frame me for makin' an attempt at your dad's life."

"Did they get Dad?" Jeff asked swiftly.

Cam shook his head. "But they will."

Jeff glanced obliquely at Murray Seth, saw the puzzlement in his face, then returned his gaze to Cam. "What happened?"

"I'll tell you first what's *goin'* to happen. They're goin' to corral the whole lot of us, Shieldses and Bollings, and throw us in jail. Then Woodring aims to get a blanket indictment for the old murder of that marshal, ship us over to another district for trial, and hang it on the lot of us."

"How do you know that?"

"He told Buck. He swapped Buck that information for information about Blackie Mayfell's death," Cam said gently. "Buck laid the killin' on you, and now Buck helps Woodring till the last Bolling is in jail, then he jumps the country. Woodring lets him."

Jeff looked at him shrewdly. "Buck never told you that."

"Not on your life," Cam said. "Buck told Lucy, even named the date when she was to leave the country. She told me, tellin' me to get out."

Jeff turned this over in his mind. It seemed likely enough, but still it came from a Shields, the greatest clan of liars in the world. He said, "What did Woodring do to you?"

"I was the next Shields scheduled to get throwed in jail," Cam said. "Pate, he's last. It all happened last night." Cam hunkered lower on his haunches, pleased with how well this was going, and took up his story. "First thing that got me suspicionin' was my rifle was took out of my room. There was another left in its place, just like it. Only it wasn't mine. Mine had my initials burned in the stock a long time ago. This one had my initials burned, too, but it was fresh." He reached around the tree, brought out Buck's carbine, and tossed it to Jeff, who examined it.

"Yeah, that burn is fresh," Jeff said noncommittally.

It should be, Cam thought; *it was burned this morning.* He went on. "That got me to wonderin' who could want my rifle. I went in town last night. Buck and Ball was at the saloon. They was talkin' about Dad gettin' killed. Ball turns to me and says, 'The gent that beefed Hagen didn't swing down from the roof to the window. He forted up on the building across the street. You want to see how he done it?' I said sure. When we went to go out, Buck was already gone, but I didn't think anything of it. We walked up the street, and Ball stops at the sheriff's office long enough to tell Woodring to take the lantern upstairs and talk to Ben because he wanted to show me how Hagen was beefed. We went across the street then to the back of that old assay office. Remember?"

"Yeah. I remember it," Jeff said slowly.

"All right. We get to the back of it, and Ball says, 'Climb up there and walk up front and you can look right into the jail.' So I done it. Ball, he never come with me. When

I gets set up there, I can see Woodring and Ben Bolling talking through the bars. I'm just ready to come down when a rifle cuts loose from the top of the next building. Somebody—and who else could it be but Buck?—shot into the jail at Ben Bolling. It never hit him, because I heard the slug smack the bars. Woodring kicked out the lantern and started shootin'." He paused a brief moment. "The funny part of it was," he said slowly, "he shot at me and hit me. He never shot at Buck."

He waited a long moment. "I got down off the other side of the roof and high-tailed it away from Ball, who started shootin' at me," he finished. He looked at them both. "Now what does that look like to you?" Jeff Bolling didn't say anything. Cam said gently, "It looks to me like Buck, on the other roof aimed to kill Ben Bolling, Woodring aimed to kill me, or if he couldn't kill me, Ball was there to get me for Bolling's murder. That would mean Bolling dead, and me dead or arrested."

"What did you do after that?" Murray Seth asked.

"I rode like hell for the ranch to get a gun and blankets. I told Lucy what happened, and then's when she told me what Buck and Woodring planned."

He let it go at that, watching them. Jeff looked quizzically at Seth, who returned his glance. Obviously they wanted to talk it over. Cam rose. "I'll tell you what I'll do, Bolling. Where you goin' now?"

"Town."

"All right, go ahead. Ask Ben what happened last night. If he tells it the way I told it, then ask Woodring what happened. See what he says. I'll be somewhere along this road this afternoon, when you come back. We can make medicine again. That all right?"

"Sure," Jeff said softly, watching Cam carefully.

Cam said, "There's just one other thing ought to convince you I ain't lyin'. I had a chance to kill you both this mornin'. I didn't. The reason I didn't is because I reckon Woodring to be a bigger enemy of mine—and yours—than all you Bollings put together. Think that over."

He turned and walked back through the timber. Jeff looked at Murray. "What do you think of that?"

"Well, he never shot us," Murray said thoughtfully.

In silence they turned and walked back to their horses. Jeff was a little uncertain of the reception he was going to get in town, but he reasoned that if Tip Woodring passed him up before, he would pass him up again. What Cam Shields had just told him served as a prod. He turned it over and over in his mind, discussing it with Murray. Certainly Cam's information about Tip Woodring fitted in with what had already happened. Hagen Shields dead, Ben Bolling arrested, and an attempt already made on his life.

In town, they put up their horses at the feed stable, and Jeff gave a kid a quarter to run up and see who was in the sheriff's office. He returned with the news that Woodring was there alone. Jeff and Murray, confident of their ability to handle anything between them that Tip could give, went up.

Tip rose at their entrance, his face belligerent. His truculence faded, however, as he saw their intentions were peaceable.

"I'd like to see Dad," Jeff said coldly. "Any law against it?"

"There ain't," Tip drawled, "but there ought to be." He put out his hand. "Give me your gun."

"Think I'm goin' to shoot him?" Jeff asked dryly.

"If you got anything to gain by it, I'm damn sure you would," Tip said bluntly. "Hand it over. Also, I'm goin' to search you."

Jeff submitted to his gun being taken and to being searched. He told Murray to stay there, and he went upstairs.

Ben came off the cot at sight of him. His face was worried, and he looked as if he hadn't slept much the night before.

"Jeff, you got to get me out of here," he said bluntly, after the greeting.

"You're scared."

"You're damn right I am!" Ben Bolling said bitterly. "I got shot at last night. I tell you, they aim to pay us back for what Murray did to Hagen Shields. I'll get it tonight or tomorrow night, I know!"

"What happened last night?"

Bolling told him. Tip had come up to talk to him. While he was standing there, somebody from the roof across the street took a shot at him.

"What did Woodring do?"

"He kicked out the lantern, shot out the window, then run downstairs and across the street. Back in the alley somewhere, they started shootin' again."

Jeff said softly, "Is that right? Who was it shot at you?"

"Woodring said it was Cam Shields. He dropped his rifle and his initials were burned on the stock. And he's loose, Jeff. He'll try it again. I tell you, if I don't get out of here, I'm a dead man! You can't guard against a man shootin' through a window!"

Jeff said gently, "You'll be out of here by tomorrow, Dad."

"How you goin' to do it?"

"I dunno," Jeff said, his eyes wicked. "Still, I'll get you out."

Jeff composed his features on his way downstairs. Tip had ordered Murray Seth to stand on the sidewalk outside the door, and from his seat at the desk he kept a watch on him.

Jeff closed the stairway door and said mildly, "Dad says somebody tried to gun him last night."

Tip nodded coolly. "Pity he was such a rotten shot."

"Who was it?" Jeff asked, disregarding the jibe.

"Cam Shields," Tip said. "He forted up on the roof of the assay office and waited until I brought the lantern into the cell block. Then he cut loose."

Jeff was watching him closely, suspicion slowly hardening into certainty. "Dad said you found the rifle."

Tip waved to the table. Jeff picked up the rifle stock,

turned it over, and saw the initials burned in the wood.
The burn was so old that it was almost the color of the
scuffed wood. He looked up at Tip. "He don't mind ad-
vertisin' he done it, does he?"

"He's not very bright."

"Like a lot of other folks around here."

Tip flushed. "All right. But from now on, that window's
goin' to be down at night and painted black."

"I didn't mean that," Jeff said pointedly.

"We'll get Cam Shields, if that's what you mean."

"I didn't mean that, either," Jeff said. He put down the
gunstock and walked out, certain as a man could be that
Cam Shields had told the truth. A cold and murderous
wrath rode him. Once he believed what Cam had told him,
he found a thousand things to bolster that belief. He was
convinced now that the real enemy of both the Bollings
and the Shieldses was Tip Woodring, with Ball a poor
second.

He wanted to see Cam Shields now, wanted to see him
right away. The ride back to the Three B was swift, a
purpose behind it.

At almost the same place in the trail, in midafternoon,
Cam Shields stepped out and hailed them. He was still
cautious enough to carry an unholstered six-gun, but he
did not demand that they drop theirs.

"Well?" he asked.

"You're right," Jeff said. "I saw your rifle. I heard Dad's
story and Woodring's, too."

Cam couldn't keep the elation out of his eyes, but he
only nodded briefly.

"You said you wanted to talk to me again. All right,
I'm listenin'."

"Let's get Woodring out of the way," Cam said calmly.

"How?"

"That's one reason why I came to you. I haven't any
men. You have."

"You reckon I ought to raid the jail?"

"You know a better way?"

"Shoot him," Murray Seth said. Immediately he was sorry he said it, because of the way Cam Shields looked at him. It was plain that Murray's two words had started Cam Shields to thinking, and Murray knew he was thinking of Hagen.

"You'll still have Ben in jail," Cam pointed out.

Jeff acknowledged that with a nod, and Cam went on. "There's Woodring and Ball and Buck that's in this," Cam said. "Woodring and Ball will be at the jail, and you'll get them and free Ben. Buck won't be no more trouble than he's always been, which is none."

"How do you know they'll be at the jail?"

Cam said, smiling, "That's where I come in. I don't expect you to do all the work, Bolling. I want in this myself." He paused. "Me, I'll just walk in there and give myself up, say, at a quarter to nine. That'll give Ball time to get Woodring there, or the other way around. They'll be sure to come and rawhide me. At nine o'clock, you walk in with your crew, and that's all there is to it."

Jeff considered this a moment, and Cam went on. "If I was you," he said carefully, "I'd have every man I could muster on hand. Start sendin' 'em in right now. Have 'em drift in in pairs, so nobody'll notice 'em. They'll be comin' in after dark and have 'em take up positions across from the jail. After I walk in and you see both Ball and Woodring there, then's the time to strike."

Jeff nodded thoughtfully.

"Every man you got," Cam said slowly, carefully. "This Woodring is a wild man. He took Ben right away from the whole lot of you. And if he's shootin', he'll be purely hell."

Jeff said slowly, "I think that'll do it."

"Whatever you do," Cam said, "get Woodring."

"We'll be there at nine."

"And I'll be there at quarter to," Cam said. He backed off into the brush and disappeared. Jeff, his arms folded on the saddle horn, regarded the timber in thoughtful silence. "Don't it seem funny to you," he said slowly, "that Cam Shields is willin' to help a Bolling?"

"I dunno," Murray scratched his head. "He hates Woodring worse than he does us, I reckon."

Jeff turned to him. "Suppose he has a bunch of gunnies planted up there in the cell block? What if he's just tryin' to toll us in to the payoff?"

Murray considered this a moment, then shook his head. "Hunh-unh. Even supposin' he had this framed with Woodring and Ball, who else could he get besides Buck and that kid? Nobody. Five agin' the lot of us."

"I don't trust him."

"Hell, neither do I. But we can't lose, Jeff—not if he tolls Woodring and Ball in there."

Jeff nodded and they rode on, presently coming out into the park in front of the house.

Cam took up his position back in the timber, where he could see the Three B. When, twenty minutes later he saw the first pair of riders cross the park and take the road to Hagen, he relaxed. It had worked, all right. He counted seven riders in all until, just before dusk, Murray Seth and Jeff Bolling rode out. Cam hunkered down, waiting, watching the house. At dark he saw a lamp being lighted in the cookshack. That, he reflected, would be the cook, and the cook alone, for according to his count every hand on the Three B and its owners were either in town or on the way.

He put his horse onto the grass of the park and made his slow way to the corrals. Dismounting there, he walked carefully toward the kitchen. The Chinese cook was standing over the stove, humming in a singsong voice that sounded weird in the night. Cam listened and could hear no other sounds.

He stepped through the doorway, his gun leveled, and the cook glanced up. His face remained inscrutable as he looked at the gun.

"Come over here, cookie," Cam drawled. The cook slowly padded over. When he was close, Cam slashed at him with the gun. The cook's arm was too slow in rising;

Cam's gun barrel rapped him over the head, and he melted to the floor. Cam went across the kitchen, looking in cupboards until he found a can of kerosene.

Then he dragged the cook out into the yard, put the kerosene down beside him, and went inside again. By considerable effort, he managed to overturn the stove. Its coals spilled out on the floor, and Cam left it. Dragging the cook over to the post where the triangle hung, he took his lariat and tied him there.

Afterward, he carried the kerosene into the main house. Walking through its rooms, he sloshed the coal oil on the floor and walls, and then, in the kitchen, touched a match to the kindling which he had laid in a kerosene-soaked clothes closet.

The rest of it was easy. The blacksmith shop, the barn, the wagon shed, and finally the corrals, after he had driven the horses out. Nothing that was made of wood was spared —and everything was timber.

Toward the last he hurried a bit, for time was pressing. Finished, he rode north across the park. Looking back, he could see the flames through the lower-floor windows of the big house. The sheds, of course, and the barn were already burning nicely, while the cookshack and bunkhouse was a little slow. But it would catch.

Turning his horse into the timber, he took the trail, a short-cut to town. According to his calculation, Jeff Bolling and Murray Seth, the last of the Three B crew, would be far over the ridge and in deep timber, both of which would screen the fire from them. As for the rest, they would be too far away to see it.

CHAPTER
10

TIP CAME OUT of the Oriental Café and turned upstreet toward the sheriff's office. Passing Baylor's Dry Goods and Grocery store, he paused to let a clerk, bowed under two sacks of flour, stagger down the steps to a buckboard at the tie rail. A girl, carrying an armful of groceries and sacks piled high enough to hide her face, followed him. The bundles were stacked so high that she missed the last step, tripped, caught herself, but recovered too late to save the bundles. They tumbled to the boardwalk, revealing Lucy Shields, an expression of exasperation on her face. She saw Tip and laughed, and Tip grinned back.

"What are you doin' in town now?" Tip demanded.

"Shopping." Lucy brushed the black wisps of hair from her face. She seemed a little pale, and her face was tense. She looked at the bundles and laughed again. "I guess I was bragging."

Tip kneeled on the boardwalk and picked up the sacks. He took hold of one and it seemed heavy to him. He fingered it and then looked up at Lucy. She was biting her lip. Carefully Tip opened the paper sack. Inside was Buck's six-gun.

Tip rose, the gun in his hand, eyeing Lucy accusingly, and Lucy laughed uneasily. "Well, I couldn't walk into a store with it in my hand. So I put it under my coat and asked for a paper sack."

Tip said, "Did Buck give this to you?"

"Yes."

Tip scowled. "You shouldn't be out this late, Lucy."

Lucy shrugged. "It's—it's Cam," she said. "Buck doesn't like to leave the place, now—and we've got to eat. Buck won't leave for long in the daytime, and not at all at night. He thinks maybe Cam will come back at night, and I'd be there alone, or with Pate."

"So he sends you to town?"

"He didn't send me to town," Lucy said loyally. "I went over to Dockstaders' this afternoon, and I figured since I was so close to town, I'd better get my shopping done. It—it was a little later than I thought."

"And you're going home now?"

"Why not? The horses know the way home."

Tip looked at her and he knew she was afraid. He felt a sudden pity for this girl, and at the same time was a little angry at her foolishness.

"You can't do it," he said firmly.

"But I've got to. They're expecting me."

"Let 'em expect. They can get their own breakfast. You'll stay in town."

"Is that an order?"

Tip nodded. "From the sheriff's office." He thought he saw Lucy relax with relief, and he said quickly, positive he was right, "I think you're glad this happened."

"I am," Lucy said quietly, looking uncertainly at Tip. "I was afraid. I—I've seen some of the Bolling crew around town, and I don't like them."

"Three B men?"

Lucy nodded. Tip said half angrily, "Then you were foolish to try and make it home."

Lucy smiled faintly. "I know it. Still, Buck and Pate run more risk than that every time they ride out."

Tip only grunted. He pointed downstreet. "You go to the hotel and stay there."

"No such thing. I'm going to see Lynn, now that I have to stay in town."

"I'll take the team down to the feed stable."

"Thanks," Lucy said. There was more color in her cheeks now, and she was pretty. She crossed the street, and Tip stood there watching her. She was a cool customer, Tip thought, the kind of a girl who sets herself a task and does it, come hell or high water. She was pretty, too; dark and warm and fresh-looking. He heard a voice say at his shoulder, "Wasn't that Lucy, Tip?"

He turned to face Lynn, and for a reason that he couldn't fathom his face felt hot. "Yes. She's headed for your place."

Lynn looked at him curiously. "Why, Tip, what have you been stealing? You're blushing."

"I've been standing on my head trying to pick up these packages."

And then Lynn, with quick intuition, understood, and she blushed, too, and turned away, saying, "Good night, Tip."

As he had done with Lucy, Tip watched Lynn cross the street. There was a difference between those two girls, he thought idly; Lynn had a grace, a swing to her walk, and the way her hair came up over her collar, leaving a few wild strands of hair curling there, was a nice thing to look at. He caught himself then, and looked guiltily around him. The clerk was picking up the sacks that had rolled into the road.

Tip took the buckboard and team down to the feed stable, his thoughts troubled. None of this was right, here. Lucy shouldn't have to carry a gun, as if she were afraid for her life. And Lynn. He realized suddenly that Lynn didn't belong here, Lynn, who had Rig Holman's money and did not have to live in this wild and savage town. Both those girls carried a burden that they couldn't share, and shouldn't be carrying. Lucy's talk drifted back through his mind. She had seen Three B men here in town, she said. For some reason that seemed curious to Tip, and he wondered what was up.

He asked the hostler, "Any Three B riders in town to-night?"

"Ain't seen any."

Upstreet, Tip dropped into the Mountain saloon. This was the dead hour, but a few men were playing cards. The bartender said he hadn't seen any of Bolling's crew. Tip went into the lobby, and it was deserted. He tried Morgan's blacksmith shop and found it closed. There weren't many places to loaf in Hagen, perhaps because Hagen had never been allowed to get in the habit of loafing. He tried the Mexican cantina down off the main street and found only a couple of transients drinking there.

Suddenly he remembered that Ball was still waiting to go to supper and he went back to the office. By the time he reached it, he had concluded that whatever Three B men were in town had ridden out by now. Still, he felt an uneasiness that would not go.

The south mail was in today, and there was a stack of newspapers on Ball's desk. Tip first went upstairs, set up his cot in the corridor, spread his blankets on it, and came down.

After that, he took off his coat, put his feet on the desk, and started looking through the newspapers. He didn't know how long he had been reading them when he heard the door open and looked up. Cam Shields, his eyes as shifty as ever, walked into the room.

"I heard you were lookin' for me," he said flatly.

Tip laid down his paper. "Who told you?"

"A rider."

Tip slowly came to his feet. "Yeah, we want you," he said. "About a hundred dollars' worth."

"What for?"

"Attempted murder."

"It's a lie, and I can prove it. Where's Ball?"

"I dunno. He'll be back, though. You can wait for him upstairs."

"Hunh-unh. I don't roost in any jail till I see Ball."

Tip smiled thinly. "That's where you're wrong, mister." He pointed to the stair doorway. "Get up them stairs."

Cam shook his head. Tip reached out to grab him, and Cam lashed out with a blow that caught Tip on the jaw and sent him back into the desk. He came off with a low growl in his throat, feinted with his right hand, then drove his left into Cam's face. Cam crashed into the table and carried it down with him.

Over the racket Tip made out the sound of many men running. He kicked the door shut, just as a shot drummed into its wood. Remembering that Cam had worn no gun, Tip forgot him. He locked the door, then picked the chair up and threw it at the lamp. It went out and crashed to the floor. Tip got a glimpse of Cam clawing to his feet. Tip flattened against the wall, palming up his gun, trying to see in that pitch-dark.

He heard men shouting outside, and it puzzled him. Who were they? They were kicking at the door now, and Tip placed a couple of shots through it. Suddenly the side window crashed out, and Tip shot in that direction. He heard a man curse softly and then back away and yell, "Give me a hand here!"

Tip thought he understood it now. These were Three B men and they had been waiting for Cam to come in, so as to get him. But how did they know he was coming? Tip whispered, "Cam, get upstairs!"

There was no answer.

Tip raced for the desk now, swung it out and against the window, then crouched in the corner as somebody systematically shot the lock off the door. Tip emptied his gun at the door, and in the ensuing silence called, "Cam!"

A sudden racket of gunfire poured in through the window, booming into the desk behind which Tip was crouched. Somebody outside was crashing at the door, battering it open. In a few seconds, Tip knew, the door would go, and then the whole lot of them would pour in on him.

He crawled to the stairway door, opened it, and from the top of the stairway a shot hammered out, its orange flash lighting up the stair well. Tip rolled to one side and lay there on the floor. He was trapped now, it seemed, by Cam and the Bollings. He crawled to his feet, raced across the room, and pushed the table and everything that was loose except the file cabinet in front of the doorway. Then he emptied his gun into the door, and the chopping stopped. He squatted against the wall then, feeling in his gun belt for fresh loads. His fingers settled on the loose cartridge loops, and he fumbled along the belt for shells. His fingers came to the last loop—and it was empty. Frantically he felt again, carefully this time, and then a black wave of despair washed over him.

He was out of shells. He lunged for the desk, pulled open the drawer where they kept the ammunition, and fumbled around among the ammunition boxes. They were all empty. He came erect, looking down in the dark at his gun. And then with a savage oath he flung it from him. He heard it hit the wall over the filing-cabinet and clatter to the floor. Out of the corner of his eye he saw a man crawling through the window. Tip picked up the swivel chair and swung it with all his might at the window. The man screamed and disappeared, and suddenly the chopping was resumed.

Tip hunkered down there, sizing up his chances, bitterly understanding what had happened. Cam Shields had thrown in with the Bollings, and this raid was to rescue Ben and to get him, Tip. Outside there was probably the whole Three B crew, while up there Cam Shields held the stairway. His only chance lay in getting up that stairway.

Outside he heard Jeff Bolling say, "Why ain't he shootin'?"

"No shells, maybe," Murray Seth said.

At that there was a renewed chopping, and Tip moved his hands frantically across the floor, looking for some kind of a weapon. And then his fingers touched the barrel of Cam Shields's broken-stock rifle. It made a wicked club as he hefted it. Then he braced himself and ran for the stairway and swung open the door. Nothing happened from the top of the stairs. Cam was gone. Tip swung the door shut behind him and battered off the knob and then took the steps two at a time. A sudden draft of air down the stairs told him that Cam Shields had shot the padlock off the roof trap door and had escaped through the roof. The lantern in the cell block to the front was still burning.

Tip called to Bolling, "I'll come back and take you again, Bolling!" on his way to the trap door. There was no answer. Suddenly suspicious, Tip stopped and raced back into the cell block. Bolling was lying sprawled on the floor, a pool of blood under his back. He had been shot.

Only the savage hammering and shooting downstairs brought Tip to his senses. Grasping his carbine barrel, his only weapon, he raced for the trap door, swung up into it just as the first man hit the stairs.

Out in the night he heard a man yell, "He's on the roof. Around in back!"

He ran along the ridgepole, slipped, fell, rolled down the roof, plummeted off, and dropped the ten feet onto the next roof. Already below him he heard a man yell, "There he went!" and a shot on the heel of it. He clawed at the roof with his free hand, but still he slipped, and then he fell again, this time between the buildings. He came down on top of a man who yelled and fought wildly. Tip kicked out savagely when he got his footing, and felt the man roll away from him. On hands and knees in the weedy passageway Tip could see two dark forms at the end of the narrow space between the two buildings. He wheeled toward the back, and came to an abrupt halt. There was another figure back there.

He heard one of the men call out, "He's in there, Jeff. Careful of Mart, though. He's down in there."

Tip hunkered down in the dark shadows, sweat beading his forehead. Something moved at his feet, and he slashed out with his club. He hit something, for he heard a groan, and the movement stopped. Slowly, hugging the wall, three men were moving in toward him.

Tip licked his lips, dragging in long breaths of air that had been pommeled out of him in the fall. A kind of wicked elation came over him now, and back of it fear was pushing. They were asking no quarter tonight, and he was giving none. He took a fresh grip on his club and then started to crawl toward the street. Ahead ten feet there was a boarded window in the saddle shop next door.

The blackness here was so dense that Tip had to feel along the wall until he found it.

Then he braced himself, his back against the jail, and kicked at the boarded window. The noise drew a racket of gunfire from both ends of the alleyway, but it was all high, for fear of hitting the Three-B hand they had called Mart.

The boards gave way and he heard something inside the building fall over with a crash. Out on the street there were people yelling, and over the din he could hear men running on the boardwalks. He crawled into the building. The light from the street came through the big windows in front.

Tip kneeled there a moment, sizing up his chances. In back they were expecting him, and doubtless there were men spread up and down the alley waiting for his break. But out in the street all was turmoil. Men Tip had seen behind store counters were running toward the jail, guns in hand. A tangle of horses blocked the street. Someone shouted, "Ain't Ball goin' to head this hunt?"

"He's back here!" someone yelled. The sound of his voice came in through the window. Tip reflected bitterly that this town was like a pack of dogs—let one dog get down, and the rest of the pack jumped on him.

He knew now that he was going to have to move, and move quickly. The back or the front? He chose the front, hoping that in the confusion he could lose himself long enough to make his escape.

Moving toward the doorway, he found it locked, then he came to the window. Men were jamming the entrance to the sheriff's office.

Tip took one last glance at the street, saw a half-dozen nervous horses at the tie rail, and made his decision. Lifting his foot, he kicked out the window, then, crouched low, crawled through it and lunged across the sidewalk. Jeff Bolling, wheeling from the entrance to the passageway between the buildings, saw him and shot. Tip tripped, sprawled between two horses, and crawled to his feet. He came up, saw a man on horseback ahead of him, and reached up and yanked him out of the saddle. He swung up into the saddle, just as a half-dozen shots raked the night. Instead of going downstreet, he pulled his horse around and crashed into the midst of the horsemen waiting. It was pandemonium. Everybody was afraid to shoot, and they slashed at Tip with their rifles. His horse was pushed against the tie rail, and Tip heard it crack and give way. He lifted the horse onto the boardwalk and roweled him through the crowd milling in front of the door to the sheriff's office. His rush knocked men sprawling, and Tip lashed out with his foot, kicking anything in his way. And then he broke free of the press, still on the sidewalk. Leaning forward over his pony's neck, he raced down the walk. Once he thought he was gone when his pony stepped through a rotten board, stumbled, and almost fell. Tip yanked him up, the shots from the posse now searching out the night around him. Out on the street, horses were racing abreast of him, riders shooting. At the first corner, still clinging to the boardwalk, Tip pulled his horse around the corner. Now they were on a cinder walk, and he sank in his spurs. Only seconds later the riders swung around the corner at full cry. Tip swung into the alley behind the jail, hoping this maneuver would throw them off, for there were men back here, too. But those riders had seen him, and they poured into the alley behind him. He ran the gauntlet of fire from the men afoot here, too, but it was a wild shooting, because these men had not known he was mounted. He scattered them at the jail, his passage drawing a scatter of shots.

Hitting the next side street, he turned back to the main street past the hotel. The posse, jammed in the narrow confines of the alley, had lost a little way, and by the time they hit the main street Tip had a whole block's advantage. They poured out after him, however, letting their guns off into the night.

As he passed the feed stable, the hostler shot at him, whether out of exuberance, because he recognized him and disliked him, or because there was a posse behind him, Tip didn't know.

He let his horse run now, knowing there was no way out of the canyon except this road. He gained a little there in the darkness, but now that he couldn't see his pursuers he felt they were closer than ever. That fear and excitement of the manhunt, old as man himself, came over him, this time with a violence that seemed to chill to the bone. For this time he was the hunted—and he didn't even have a gun.

At the opening of the canyon Tip cut across the park, forded the creek, and was almost into the timber when the posse came out. He knew they would spread out in groups, working the ground between the few scattered roads. As soon as daylight came they would pick up his tracks, and then close in on him. The thing to do, the only thing to do if he wanted to live, was to head for the peaks, traveling in a straight line and riding hard.

When Jeff Bolling, on Tip's heels, climbed the stairs to the cell block, he paused and glanced at his father's cell. Murray Seth came after him. They paused, motionless, and looked at Ben Bolling's body. Downstairs, the racket was thunderous, but here it was quiet.

Murray spoke first, softly. "That dirty double-crosser of a Cam Shields. We were crazy, Jeff."

Jeff's face, tight and wicked and baleful, didn't change. He said, "How do you know it was Cam?"

"Who else came up here besides Cam? Woodring. All right. He was out of shells, wasn't he?"

Jeff lifted a hand to his gun belt and flipped three shells onto the floor and then looked up at Murray. "Now do you think Woodring was out of shells?"

Murray stared at him. "You mean you'll hang it on—"

"Hell, yes, I will!" Jeff blazed. "Woodring is the man we've got to lick! Cam killed Dad, of course. We were suckers enough to fall for his story! But we'll use this to hang Woodring higher than a kite! Get downstairs, quick, and let me take care of this!"

One of the Three B crew raced up the stairs and Murray yelled, "Get up on the roof, you fool!" The man raced up the ladder without looking at the cell block. Murray and Jeff exchanged the briefest of glances, and then Murray plunged down the stairs, Jeff on his heels. Jeff stopped at the passageway, listening to his men call back and forth through that passageway that held Tip Woodring. A wild desire to go in there after him rode Jeff Bolling for a moment, but a look at that dark strip and knowledge that it held a wickedly dangerous man stopped him. He flattened against the wall, throwing shots into the darkness. He heard the noise of smashing wood, and paused to listen. Then, to one side of him on the boardwalk, he heard a window jangle brokenly, and wheeled.

He had only a glimpse of Tip Woodring lunging for the protection of the horses, and he shot wildly. After that it was bedlam. He fought to get out in the street, and was run down by a rider and knocked sprawling. He had only the briefest glimpse of a man crashing through the tie rail, while everyone was shouting and shooting, and then the mob flowed past him.

Hauling himself to his feet, he saw Ball racing for the jail. He ran to meet him, fury in his white face.

"Damn you, Ball, come with me!"

He hauled Ball around by the coat and shoved him into the jail. Upstairs, Jeff paused beside the cell, pointing at Ben Bolling's body. He was breathing hard, as if he were going to choke before he could speak.

"Look at that!" he ground out. "You're sheriff, Ball! Look at it!" He was almost screaming with fury. A dozen men, one or two of them Three-B riders, formed a loose circle around Ball.

"I see it," Ball said weakly. "Who done it?"

Jeff said savagely, "Who done it! Why, damn you, Woodring done it! Who else could?"

Ball only stared stupidly at him. Some townsman who had been in the street said, "I thought Woodring was out of shells?"

Jeff wheeled and pointed to the three shells he had dropped on the floor. "Does that look like he was out of shells? Hell, his gun was only empty. He come up here, loaded up in front of Ben, and then killed him! He was in such a hurry to get the butcherin'-job over that he dropped these." Something broke inside Jeff Bolling then. He lunged at Ball, grabbing his coat in his fist, and shoved him against the bars. "Why, you murderin', hammer-headed son, you let him do it! You told him to do it!"

Ball gagged out a denial, but Jeff Bolling seemed out of his mind. He threw Ball to the floor and kicked him. Ball came up fighting, only to be clubbed behind the ear by one of the Three B hands. A kind of madness was in these men, an unreasoning lust for violence and a victim, and Jeff Bolling's fury seemed to touch it off. Ball climbed to his feet, and Jeff knocked him down again. That time Ball tried to get up and couldn't. Jeff hauled him to his feet and hit him in the face and then threw him to the floor again.

"You're through, Ball," he said thickly. "Get out of here before I shoot you."

Ball headed for the stairs, and Jeff kicked him down them. In his wrecked office Ball came unsteadily to his feet. There were townsmen in the room, men Ball had known all his life, and he looked at them appealingly.

"Throw this crew out," he demanded. "I need help."

But the sympathy tonight was all with Bolling. Nobody knew who started the fight, and nobody took the trouble to ask. All they knew was that Ben Bolling was dead, murdered in his cell, and they assumed that Tip Woodring had killed him, thus starting the fight. Ball's appeal for help met with a cold reception.

Somebody said, "You're a hell of a sheriff, Ball! That's all I got to say!"

Jeff swung Ball around, nearly yanking him off his feet. "I'll tell you what you're goin' to do, Ball. You're goin' to deputize us to organize a posse that will hunt that killer down and hang him to the highest cottonwood in Vermilion county! Start doin' it."

Ball looked around the crowd again. Jeff Bolling hit him again, knocking him into the desk.

Ball said quietly, "Be damned to the lot of you! Tip Woodring never shot Bolling."

Ball went down under a dozen blows, and mercifully he did not feel them. They left him there lying on the floor in a pool of blood, while they milled out into the street, running for horses to join the posse and the manhunt. Hell with law!

When Ball opened his eyes he was lying with his cheek across the floor. Slowly the room came into focus, and there, straight ahead of him under the big filing-cabinet, was a gun. Ball knew only the need for that gun, and he tried to crawl toward it. But before he reached it he blacked out.

It was Lynn and Lucy Shields who found Ball, and with Anna's help took him to their rooms and called Dr. Pendexter. And while Doc worked on Ball, cleaning his cuts and bandaging his ribs and setting his arm, which had been broken in the fall downstairs, he told Lynn what he had heard of this night's happenings.

"They're mad," Lynn said softly when Doc was finished talking. "Tip Woodring wouldn't kill a man that way."

Dr. Pendexter straightened up. "Young lady," he said, "you can't live around hate for years without taking a little of it to yourself. That's what this town did. Tonight they've seen a murder and been told the name of the man who did it. They'll hunt him down and hang him, and a year later they won't know why they did it."

"Hang him?" Lynn said softly.

"Yes, ma'am. If they find him. And they'll find him, unless he's a mighty smart man."

"He is mighty smart."

"But not smart enough to stay away from this town. Not smart enough that, once he come into it, he couldn't keep his mouth shut. And not smart enough, once he opened his mouth, not to ask help from these people. Tonight, they found out they hated him because he was a better man than they are. Well, he'll have to prove it. Personally, I wouldn't want the job."

CHAPTER
11

CAUTION TOLD TIP TO CLEAR OUT of this country. High in the peaks country, hunkered down behind a boulder for warmth against the night wind, he counted his chances. He had a dozen matches, no gun, no food, no blankets, no ammunition. Around him, he knew, these men were beating the country. If they didn't turn him up in two days their anger would abate. Impersonal anger can seldom stand inconvenience, Tip knew, and these people had no personal interest in hunting him down. He thought back over the evening, and it was like a nightmare. The first of it, the raid by the Bollings—an attempt to free Ben, he supposed—was to be expected. But the posse, lynch-mad and in a killing mood. Of course, the word had got out that he had killed Ben Bolling. But why did they care? It was one of those times when people, caught with a lust for killing, never stopped to ask questions—only acted. In that short while all the work he had done here, all the impartial justice he had tried to deal out to both sides, had been wiped out. It was worse than if it had never existed, for now Jeff Bolling, with the sympathy of the town with him, would make short work of the Shieldses.

He shivered there in the night, thinking of Buck and Pate and Lucy. Buck would hear of it, size up the temper of the town and the Bollings, and be warned, he hoped. And meanwhile Cam Shields was loose. Strangely enough, Tip felt no anger against Cam Shields. He had lived up to his stature, which Tip had always known was small. Cam Shields would have to be hunted down and shot, killed. He was like a mad dog who communicates his madness to other dogs, until there is no end to the harm that one isolated act had started.

From down the slope he heard the report of a gunshot drifting across the wind. He listened, a kind of sadness taking hold of him. Up there and over the peaks there was a peace of sorts. Down here was red murder and misery and work and danger, and maybe death. But down here lay salvation for him, and peace for all his friends. Lynn Mayfell, troubled and helpless and stubborn; Lucy and Buck and Pate, needing help now more than ever—and Ball. They were all down there, a part of his life now.

He turned up the collar of his coat and walked over to his horse. After staking out his strange pony with the lariat he found slung over the horn, he scratched the gray's ears for a few moments, trying to make up for the grueling treatment he had given him. Afterward he came back to his rock, lay down, and looked up at the stars. He was going to stay, he decided. He was going to do it all over again, and this time he would make it stick; and bitterness had its lonely way with him.

At dawn he was down in the timber again, traveling toward the Bridle Bit. His pace was slow, for he was weaponless, and he took advantage of each eminence to scan the country below him. Once, traveling a gully that was unavoidable, he pulled into the brush at the sound of riders. Four men passed him, silent, gray-faced with exhaustion. They were so sleepy that they rode over his tracks without noticing them.

He worked deeper into the timber, feeling as if he were walking into a trap. Presently he came out on the tip of a mesa which overlooked the Three B. Tip could see its smoking ruins, with nothing standing save the stone chimney of the big house. Was that Cam, too?

Sick at heart, Tip turned away from the sight of it, and rode on through the timber, keeping to the ridges. It was midmorning before he was on Bridle Bit land, and he knew that now he would have to be careful, for they would expect him here. With an infinite caution, stopping to listen minutes at a time, he worked his way to the edge of the timber that flanked the Bridle Bit.

And what he saw there at the Bridle Bit confounded him. There were thirty horsemen or so gathered around the yard. Some of the men were dismounted, others were still in the saddle. Lucy and Buck, on the step, were listening to a man talking to them from horseback. Tip thought it was Joerns, over at the bank. He could pick out Jeff Bolling, listening peaceably enough, and Baylor and some of the more substantial citizens. And Lynn was leaning against the house next to Lucy, taking it all in.

It was Joerns's idea, so Jeff let him talk. They had overtaken Lynn Mayfell and Lucy on the ride out, and there wasn't much said until they arrived at the Bridle Bit. When Buck saw this mob and identified some of its members, he leaned his rifle against the jamb and came to the door to meet them. His glance at Lucy was quizzical and relieved, but it was Jeff Bolling he watched, hoping to get a clue from his expression.

Joerns, dressed in solid black, was a jowly man who took the weight of his affairs with a gravity that became them. Buck was surprised to find a man who usually kept aloof from the feud and its people in the vanguard of this mob. What was it, a posse?

Joerns pulled up and said, "Good morning," gravely, and Buck returned his greeting. Lucy dismounted, as did Lynn, and came over to him.

"Buck, where is Cam?" Joerns began.

"He's been kicked off this place," Buck said quietly. "You'd know that, Joerns, if you took the trouble to ask."

"And Woodring?"

"I don't know."

Lucy plucked warningly at his sleeve and Buck looked at her, puzzled.

Joerns said gravely, "You haven't heard, I suppose, that Woodring murdered Ben Bolling in his cell last night and then escaped the posse that took out after him?"

Buck shook his head. "I don't believe it."

"What you believe about the facts doesn't change them,"

Joerns said dryly. "You were a friend of his, weren't you?"

"I was and I still am," Buck said, truculence coming into his voice. He looked from Joerns to Baylor to the smug, baleful face of Jeff Bolling, and then asked, "What are you doin', arrestin' me because I knew him?"

"Not that," Joerns said. He shifted in his saddle. "Buck, some of us in this town have never liked this Bolling-Shields feud. We've tolerated it for a long time, principally because we didn't care to risk our necks in taking sides. But when a man is murdered in our own jail by a bullying deputy sheriff, it's time we took a stand."

"I've thought that for a long time," Buck said, looking at Bolling.

"You don't have to think it any more," Joerns said sharply. "That's what we're telling you now. This feud is going to stop." He paused, looking sternly at Buck. "Those aren't just words, either. We're going to stop it."

"How?"

"You're going to move out of this county, Buck—you and all your family, with all your belongings."

Buck stared at him in disbelief. Buck was always slow to anger, and he realized immediately that he must be slower than ever now.

"You can't do that, Joerns," he said calmly. "I'm a property holder in this county, entitled to the protection of the law. If I remember correct, it was my old man that brought you in here, Joerns. I've got more right here than you have."

"We're not talking about right, Buck. You've forfeited whatever right you earned. You've got to get out."

"But why us?" Buck asked, his voice a shade harder. "Why not the Bollings?"

"Because your man in the sheriff's office murdered Ben Bolling last night," Joerns said calmly. "Because you or your men burned the Three B to the ground last night. And finally, because this town would rather have the Bollings here than the Shieldses and their hired lawmen! Is that reason enough?"

"Not near enough," Buck said. "You think I'm goin' to lose this spread because you've finally taken sides in Hagen?"

"You won't lose the spread," Joerns said. "This place will be put up for auction by the bank, and you'll get the money from the sale. We're not asking you to lose your stake here, Buck. We're just telling you to move it—*telling* you, understand?"

"Nobody will buy this place without a title And I'm not signin' any deed, Joerns."

"I think you are," Joerns said calmly. "You remember that marshal who came in here and was killed, Buck? Well, maybe you didn't know it, but you killed him. I am one witness to the murder, and Baylor is the other, and we've got enough men here to take you to the U. S. Commissioner."

Lynn spoke up then, and her voice was low with contempt. "For anybody who claims to be a man, Mr. Joerns, that's the lowest, most cowardly, and despicable thing a man can do!"

Joerns flushed and looked sharply at Lynn. "It may be cowardly, Miss Stevens, but it's sense."

"Why don't you put them both out of the county then?" Lynn cried hotly. "If one's guilty, so is the other!"

"I've told you," Joerns said angrily. "Maybe there wasn't any choice before, but when Buck joined up with this crooked lawman, that's a little too much. At least the Bollings kept their fight to themselves and away from us. The Shieldses tried to corrupt our law, frame Ben Bolling with a murder he couldn't possibly have committed, and then, when they saw he was about to be taken away from them, they shot him. That's enough, we say. They're going!"

He glared angrily at Lynn, as if trying to frighten her into silence. Then he looked at Buck. "Well, what will it be, Buck? Will you go or will you stand trial for the murder of a marshal?"

"If you think by makin' me move Lucy and Pate out of

this county and give up the spread, you'll settle this fight, you're loco!" Buck said grimly. "I still got a horse, and I still got some money to buy shells!"

"That's your risk," Joerns said. "But maybe you'll think twice when I tell you that the moment you set foot over the county line, there'll be a reward of twenty-five hundred dollars on your head, on Tip Woodring's, and Cam Shields's, too!"

Buck took a step toward Joerns, and Lucy caught him by the arm. He looked at her as if he didn't recognize her and then he listened to her say, "Come in the house a minute, Buck."

Lucy and Lynn and Buck went inside and shut the door. Buck looked at Lucy and said thickly, "Hell, I'll stand trial before I'll give up this place!"

"Buck, think a minute," Lucy pleaded. "The Shieldses have got a bad name now, in the commissioner's office. And if two respectable men like Joerns and Baylor swear you killed that marshal, you'll hang!"

"I don't give a damn!"

"Yes, you do, Buck," Lynn said gently. "As long as you're alive, you can get the place back. But not in jail or dead."

It was the hardest thing Buck Shields ever faced, Lynn knew. Everything in him protested against it, but Lynn thought he would give in. And he did, after a moment of furious thought that made his face ugly with anger.

"All right," he said grimly, briefly.

Joerns was called in. He had the deed already prepared, and Buck signed it without a word.

It was Lucy who spoke to Joerns. "How much time have we?"

"Till sundown. We'll help you, and we'll escort you to the county line." He walked to the door and called, "Give a hand here, you men. You'd better scare up a couple of spring wagons, too."

"Ours will be enough," Lucy said quietly. "You see, we'll be back, Joerns. We'll travel light, because we'll be back."

Buck looked at her gratefully and turned away. Lucy went into the house, refusing the help of anyone except Lynn. Pate, coming back from Dockstaders' where he had been sent to get Lucy, was told the news and he accepted it, taking his cue from Buck. Some of the posse left for town, but more than a dozen men loafed around the wagon shed, waiting to escort the Shieldses to the county line.

They were ready by midmorning with one spring wagon holding their bedding, clothes, food, some grain, and a tarp.

Buck came in and looked around the house, speculating on what more they needed. His face was set in a grim cast, patience masking whatever he thought.

Lynn came up to him and said, "Have you an extra horse, Buck?"

"Lots of 'em," Buck said. "But we aren't goin' your way, Lynn."

"I'm going yours," Lynn said simply. "Will I be in the way, or can I help, Buck?"

Buck frowned at her. "You mean, you want to go with us?"

"I do." She smiled. "I think I know exactly what you're going to do, Buck. You'll camp just over the line, and you won't move from there until you get this place back. Am I right?"

"Right."

"Then you can use me. Will you take me?"

Buck smiled and said simply, "It'll be tough, Lynn."

"Of course it will. But no tougher on me than on you and Lucy and Pate." She laughed shakily. "I've got my fighting blood up, Buck. I can understand how Tip felt now. I wish I had his temper."

Buck grinned and went out. Lynn wanted to ask him what he thought of Tip's chances, and where he thought Tip was. But she understood that Buck was thinking the same things, content to believe that Tip was innocent of any crime until he admitted it himself.

They started off before noon on their slow trek to the county line. Pate went on ahead with the loose horses. Buck drove the wagon, and Lucy and Lynn rode on either side of it. They went south to the end of the park and took the road west. Buck didn't even look back at the place, and neither did Lucy. Lynn knew that neither of them were admitting to themselves that the Bridle Bit was lost to them. By all rights, Lynn thought, they should have been glad to leave it, with its history of bloodshed and sadness and violence. But it was home, something that had been fought for and would be fought for again.

It was after dark when they came to the county line, marked only by a blazed tree that seemed to be recognized by most of them. Buck pulled past it, then stood up in the wagon and surveyed the bulking shadows of the horsemen behind him.

"Well, boys," he drawled, "I'll see you tomorrow."

"Come on over, Buck," one voice taunted. "You're worth twenty-five hundred to us on this side of that tree."

"In about a week I'll be worth ten thousand."

The riders turned back, and Buck set about pitching camp. They pulled off into a clearing, and while Lucy and Lynn built a fire, Buck and Pate put up a rope corral and drove the horses into it. A tarp shelter was thrown up, and Buck and Pate were lugging in wood for the night's fire.

Lynn heard them dragging it in, and paid no attention. When she looked up, it was to see Tip Woodring dump an armload of wood on the pile.

She came slowly to her feet, not believing her eyes, and then she cried, "Tip!"

Buck heard her and from out in the darkness let out a whoop of joy. Pate came running behind him, and Lucy almost lost the biscuit dough in the fire.

Tip stood there smiling. He was unshaven, and his clothes were torn, and his leg was stiff with the old wound, but there was a kind of defiance about him, a strength and confidence that warmed Lynn and made her glad.

Tip only offered the information that he had shaken

the posse, had watched the eviction, and had followed them all the afternoon. When supper was laid out on the grass, Tip wolfed it as if he were starved. Afterward, with Buck's gun handy, with his pipe going, the fire blazing, and the pines overhead stirring and whispering in the night wind, Tip told the story of the fight at the jail, beginning with Cam's entrance.

When he was finished, Buck said gently, "So it was Cam? And Jeff Bolling knew that. He saw Cam talkin' to you."

"He sent him, I reckon," Tip said, frowning. "But I don't get it all. Jeff knew Cam made his try for Ben, because I told him."

"And Cam burned the Three B?" Lynn asked.

"I didn't and Buck didn't," Tip said. "There's only Cam left."

They talked of other things then, of the town's sudden uprising against Tip and the Shieldses, and of Anna Bolling, alone in town now with Ball, hating her brothers and everything they stood for. Buck didn't join in the talk of Anna, keeping silent and listening, his face a little sad. When it was time to turn in, Buck and Tip and Pate went over to the wagon for the bedding.

"What are we going to do, Tip?" Buck asked.

"Fight."

"A whole county? Hell, that's what I thought there at the spread. But this afternoon I began thinking what a job that was. Where do we begin?"

"I can tell you that, too," Tip said quietly. "We begin with Cam. We can forget the rest until he's out of the way. I'm going to hunt him down and kill him first. After that I'm goin' to get Jeff Bolling. After that, I'll go in that town and knock some sense into their heads, and get Ball on his feet. And after that, Buck, we'll get your place back."

"*We'll* do all that?"

Tip laughed. "You and me."

They lugged the bedding back to the fire, and Lynn and Lucy made up the beds. When they were all settled, Buck and Pate in the wagon, Lucy and Lynn by the fire, and Tip off under the trees, Tip couldn't sleep. He rolled out of the blankets, pulled on his boots, loaded his pipe, and walked off to the edge of the clearing. It was a cool night, the stars icy spikes in the high night sky. Tip looked up at them, wondering if they had ever looked down on more confusion and misery and hard luck than had been assembled around that campfire tonight.

Suddenly he heard someone walking across the grass, and Lynn appeared at his side.

"I followed the smell of your pipe smoke," Lynn said. "I couldn't sleep."

"There's too much waiting to be done."

Lynn didn't speak for a moment, then said, "You're a pretty loyal friend, aren't you, Tip?"

"I've been thinkin' the same about you," Tip replied. "You didn't have to follow them out here."

"But I'm different. There's no threat over my head."

"There's none over mine," Tip answered quickly. "I don't call a tinhorn's brag a threat."

Lynn laughed. "You'll never change, will you, Tip?"

"I don't reckon," Tip answered slowly, "even if you'd like to see me."

"But I wouldn't. Once, a long time ago, that was, I thought you were hotheaded and rash and a little too tough for your own good."

"Maybe I am."

"No. That was a long time ago, I said. I've changed my mind. I changed it today, I think, when I understood how heartless and cowardly and small some men can be."

Tip didn't say anything.

"Lucy and Buck's trouble makes ours look rather small, doesn't it?"

Tip said with wry humor, "Mine may be small, but they're mine." He looked at Lynn, only a dark shape in the night beside him. "Blackie Mayfell must have been a pretty good father, wasn't he?"

"He was the best," Lynn said simply, adding, "Why did

you say that, Tip?"

Tip answered in his oblique fashion. "A man will do anything for money, Lynn. Look at me. I've got myself shot and now they're huntin' me, and all I'd have to do to get away from it would be to say good-by to ten thousand dollars I hope I can get. You, you're doin' this for a reason—the right reason—and it makes me some ashamed of my own."

Lynn said quietly, "You don't understand yourself, Tip."

"I always thought I did."

"You've been telling yourself all along that you're doing this to earn money. You started out with that in mind. But that isn't what brought you back here today, and it isn't what'll keep you here. You're doing it for Buck and Lucy." She hesitated. "And sometimes, I almost think you're doing a little of it for me. If you are, Tip, thanks."

She walked away, leaving Tip confounded.

When Lynn crawled into her blankets, Lucy stirred. "Who is it?"

"Lynn."

Lucy said, "Oh," and Lynn waited a moment, then said, "I was talking to Tip. He couldn't sleep, either."

"Yes, I know. Good night, Lynn."

Lynn caught the note of wistfulness in Lucy's voice, and she pitied her. Lucy was a closemouthed girl, but some things about her were more eloquent than speech. Lynn had watched her, feeling a small pang of jealousy, when she looked at Tip. Something softened in Lucy then, and her eyes shone with a sadness that none of these men seemed to notice. Lynn knew what it was, because she felt that way herself when she looked at Tip.

She turned over in her blankets, angry with herself and a little sorry for herself, too.

CHAPTER

12

At dawn next morning Tip and Buck rolled out of their blankets, saddled their horses, divided their guns and shells, and rode out into the chill of early morning, heading for the Bridle Bit. Tip figured that Cam, on the prowl as he himself had been only yesterday, would soon come across the sign of riders heading for the Bridle Bit, and curiosity would take him to the ranch.

He and Buck kept off the road, making a wide circle from camp before they crossed the county line. Bounty hunters, with five thousand dollars in reward money as incentive, would be combing this country with a vengeance.

At the Bridle Bit they kept in the timber until they had examined the house thoroughly. It was deserted, with no sign of life. Without the stock in the corrals, it looked as if it had not been lived in for years. Tip took one side of the house and Buck took the other, and they began their search for Cam's tracks. Buck knew Cam's horse, knew its tracks, too, and they worked from this. The going was slow, trying to pick one track from those of the thirty horses.

Presently, from the yard, Buck whistled, and Tip rode around the house to him.

"Been here this mornin'," Buck said, pointing to the ground. "There's frost in the others, or else they're wet where the sun's melted it. But those tracks are Cam's and you can see where the wet dirt is balled under the shoe and dry dust in the tracks."

Tip nodded. Once spotted, the tracks were easy to follow across the wet grass of the park. In the timber, the cover of pine needles was an even better giveaway, but Tip reserved judgment. When Cam learned that he was being followed, he would take pains to cover his tracks, and then the going would be slow.

Cam was keeping to cover like a skulking wolf, and heading for the Bolling place. Presently they came to the place he had dismounted to look at the Three B. Beyond the ruins of the house which were still smoking in the thin morning air, there were several tents pitched. Off in the timber the steady *chonk-chonk* of working axes was audible.

"Jeff's goin' to stick it out, too," Tip murmured.

"Hell, he's got the county behind him," Buck said. "Why shouldn't he?"

"A damn good reason. He won't be alive to see it finished."

Mounting again, they followed Cam's tracks. He was keeping just into the timber, circling the park. He rounded the north end, and then came back on the east side, riding in the direction of the axmen. As they came closer, Tip grew cautious. Cam was taking a risk now, getting this close to the workmen. Tip pulled up and Buck came up to him.

"What's he up to?" Buck asked. "He's too damned much of a coward to—"

Crack!

A rifle's sharp slam cut the woodchopping dead. A man yelled up ahead, and then Tip roweled his horse.

"That's Cam!" Tip cried. "Stick to his tracks, Buck."

He raced on through the timber in the direction of a shot. Far ahead, he saw a horse shuttling through the timber. Tip sent a snap shot in that direction that buried itself in a tree somewhere ahead. Buck pulled off to one side and raced abreast Tip. When they picked up the tracks of Cam's horse, Tip yelled again, "Stick to the tracks, Buck. I'll try to ride him down."

He cut off through the timber, listening for the sound of Cam's horse, but the floor of pine needles smothered every sound. Behind him he could hear men yelling across the park to the tents.

Tip caught one more glimpse of a rider far ahead through the trees, and he shot again and missed. Cam was slanting up the slope at a dead run.

Tip swung in toward him, and presently came to a *cienega*. He started across it just as Cam, across the park, opened fire. The grass in front of his horse ripped up with the tearing sound of sod, and Tip yanked his horse back into the brush. Keeping to the timber he circled the park and came to the place where Cam had halted to shoot.

Up ahead he could hear rock sliding, and put his horse into a lope through the trees. He arrived in a clearing just in time to see Cam disappear over a rocky ridge. Tip put his horse to it, and then, as he saw Cam's head appear over the rim, yanked him back and raced for the timber. Cam laid shots all around him, and before he reached the trees he got a sliver of rock in his cheek. He dismounted in the shelter of the brush and pulled his rifle out of the scabbard, bellied down, and started to return Cam's shots. Once he turned and saw Buck plunging up through the timber, and he waved him back and made a wide circle with his arm. Buck nodded and disappeared in the timber off to the right. Tip kept firing, and Cam was laying his shots closer now. Some of Cam's panic seemed to have vanished and he was shooting carefully.

Presently, from off the right on the ridge, Buck's rifle cracked out once. Tip saw Cam rise and look, and he took a quick shot. Cam's head disappeared, and Buck began to shoot again. There was a scrabble of hoofs on rock, and Tip leaped into the saddle and roweled his horse up the slope.

He and Buck met at the top, and Buck said, "I hit him, I think. He's runnin' now."

Cam headed down-slope now for the timber, riding in a straight line. Tip, after telling Buck to stick to the tracks, made a wide circle off into the timber, riding hard. Presently he swung back, riding carefully and listening. He had made three quarters of his circle, and still he heard and saw nothing. He backtracked now, and still did not pick up Cam's tracks. Completing the circle and coming out at the edge of the timber, he saw Buck had gone. He shot three times, and from up the hill a half mile came Buck's answering shots.

Tip swore softly and put his horse up the slope. Cam had kept his head, entering the timber, skirting its edge, and then angling up the mountain, while he had wasted time in his circle and Buck had wasted time in the slow business of tracking.

Later, when Tip caught up with Buck, Cam was headed in a straight line for the rocky country up the slope and ahead.

"This means a hunt, Tip," Buck said gloomily.

"We can last as long as he can. Come on."

They agreed that Tip should ride out ahead, once the general direction Cam was traveling was settled on. By making wide circles, Tip might be able to pick up the tracks and save hours of painstaking tracking. Also, it might serve to flush out Cam from a hiding-place or crowd him into being careless. At any rate, nothing would be lost, for Buck would stick to his tracks, and Buck was as adept at tracking as Cam was at covering them.

It was a slow business at best, however. Tip and Buck took turns on the tracking. Cam had his head now, and he was coolly and systematically trying every shift he knew to throw them off the trail. Buck, riding ahead, got a glimpse of him in early afternoon, but it was too far to shoot. The country was one of canyons and upthrust mesas above Hagen. Buck summoned Tip with three shots. By this lucky chance, they had killed Cam's chance for a wide circle around them and into the timber up the slope. To be sure of it, Buck emptied his rifle at Cam, and saw him turn down again for the shelter of the canyons below.

When Tip rode up, Buck pointed out the place where he had seen Cam. "He's movin' down from there."

Tip nodded. "We better split up soon."

"Why?"

"We're bein' followed," Tip said quietly. "Bolling is on our trail now. I saw his men twice, but they didn't see me."

Buck swore softly, and put his horse down the gravelly slope into the arroyo. When they came to where Cam had paused, they saw small brown spots on the sand. It was blood, already dried by the heat of the sand. They swung west then, down the slope, traveling the same arroyo Cam had chosen. Buck was looking about him now, studying the country. Presently he pulled up.

"Tip, I'm goin' to take a chance."

"On what?"

"This gut forks and empties into the canyon above Hagen. Cam's only got one chance to dodge the town and that's by goin' out of the canyon on the other side. If I can beat him to it, I can bottle him up there. He'll be afraid to go back, because he'll figure he'll run into you. But instead of waiting, you swing out and come out below town. You move in and I move in and we'll have him in town."

"Will he go there?"

"He's hurt, and the chances are he will. Besides, his horse is wore down and he'll hit for town, anyway, to steal a fresh one."

Tip nodded and named a meeting-place, and then climbed out of the arroyo at the first opportunity. It was slow traveling here, for the country was slashed by narrow canyons and capped by a loose shale that was treacherous footing. Below, the timber looked green and inviting, and he knew that Cam would choose it, rather than this country. And beyond the timber was the canyon, and in it the town. A wounded man would head for it by instinct, trusting to the night to hide his presence.

It was dark when Tip finished his circle and put his horse down into the canyon mouth below town, then traveled the road. Presently he pulled his horse into the brush and hunkered down to wait, like an Indian. He wasn't hungry and he wasn't tired, and there seemed to

be no room for either in his mind. He speculated on where
they would catch up with Cam, if he had the good luck to
dodge them that night. But he wouldn't, Tip knew. He
didn't know how he knew, but he was certain. Tonight his
score with Cam would be settled.

Darkness came, and only a lone puncher, one of the
Dockstader boys, passed him. Afterward, Tip pulled out
of the brush and headed for town. In the deep shadows of
the graveyard, where Hagen Shields was buried, he caught
Buck's whistle.

"He's in town," Buck said. "I turned him back down
the canyon. I think he was headed for the lower country."

"What about Bolling?"

"He's in town now, too."

Tip said gently, "Well, well. Maybe this will be a bigger
night than we expected."

He and Buck moved toward town then, and sought the
darkness of the alley that ran behind the feed stable. In
the rear of the hotel they left their horses and hunkered
down against the wall for a conference. Cam was in town,
but where?

"Who does he know here, Buck?"

"Nobody that wouldn't like to see him dead," Buck
said briefly.

"No friends? Nobody that would hide him out?"

"Not even the Mexicans for money."

"Then we'll start combin' the alleys for him. I'll start at
the north end and you start at the south. Look in the loft
of the feed stable if you can. And I'll look in Doc Pendexter's office. And be careful, Buck."

They separated then. The job, while it sounded difficult,
really wasn't, Tip thought. Wedged in the canyon the
way it was, Hagen had only three streets, two cross streets,
and two alleys.

Tip started at the north end of town. He was thorough
and quiet, but the darkness hampered him. Cam Shields
could have been hiding in any one of the dozen woodsheds
he had examined, but it would be suicide to light a match.

Twice riders came down the alley and Tip slipped into the shadows, letting them pass.

When he had worked his way into the heart of town, he was discouraged. He kept thinking of Doc Pendexter, but he wanted to exhaust all the other possibilities first. But when he came to Baylor's warehouse and found it unlocked, he knew it was hopeless. If Cam Shields could find hiding-places like this, he could stay there for weeks without being discovered. In desperation then, he turned into the passageway between the assay office and the barbershop, over which Dr. Pendexter had his office. The stairway to it was covered, which meant that he would have to approach it from the street.

At the edge of the boardwalk, Tip paused and scanned the street. The sheriff's office, across the street and a few doors up, was lighted, and several men loafed about the door. That would be Bolling, he supposed, and his riders.

When the boardwalk was clear, Tip slipped out and wheeled into the covered stairway. He climbed it cautiously, two steps at a time, his gun in his hand.

The door at the top was solid, and he put his ear to it. There was a lamp lighted inside, but the room was silent. Turning the knob, he stepped into the room, and closed the door with a noise. He was standing in an empty waiting-room. Hearing footsteps, he turned to a door in the side wall. It opened to reveal Dr. Pendexter in shirt sleeves, a book in his hand. He looked at Tip a long time, as if trying to remember him.

"Oh, yes, I bandaged your leg," Dr. Pendexter said calmly.

"Know me, Doc?"

"Of course." He frowned at the gun. "If you think I'm interested in getting twenty-five hundred dollars, I'm not," Doc said dryly. "I am, I should say, but I'm not interested in getting it that way. Come in." He stepped aside. Tip went into his office, looking carefully around him as Doc closed the door behind him. His face was alert, strained, and Doc put it down to a natural caution.

"Leg troubling you?"

"No," Tip said. He swung his gaze full on Dr. Pendexter, and said, "It's not for me, Doc. I'm after information."

"Ah," Doc said, and Tip's glance sharpened.

"You've guessed," he said. "Has he been here?"

"Who?"

"Cam Shields."

Doc didn't say anything. Tip's glance traveled the room, settled on the wastebasket which held soiled bandages still red with blood. He looked briefly at Doc and then went to the door. Opening it, he saw a faint trace of blood on the waiting-room floor. In the office, it had already been cleaned up. He shut the door and lowered his gun under Doc's untroubled gaze. Then he sat on the arm of a chair and pulled out his pipe. He didn't pack it, only rubbed it thoughtfully, bringing out the gloss of the grain.

"Well?" Doc said sharply.

"I'm just tryin' to think of an argument," Tip said carefully, and looked from the pipe to Doc. "I'm tryin' to think of a good reason why you should protect a killer like Cam Shields."

Doc laughed shortly. "Aren't you goin' to take your gun and threaten me?"

"Why should I?" Tip said. "That never settled anything. You'll tell me if you want to, and you won't if you don't want to. I reckon there's nothin' I can do that will make you."

"You have more sense than some people who have been here lately."

"How lately?" Tip asked softly.

"Ten minutes ago, maybe."

"How bad was he hit?"

"Bad enough so he can't travel far."

Tip regarded Doc with a level stare. "As far as some woodshed close?"

"Damn it!" Doc said. "A doctor has some secrets. I can't tell you."

"And I can't hunt him unless you do," Tip countered. "Did you know he killed a man today, shot him in the back as the man was cutting logs? Do you know he killed Ben Bolling? Do you know he'll kill you when he finds out I came here?"

"Don't scare me," Doc said derisively.

"I'm not scaring you. I don't think I could. I'm only tellin' you the truth. For a couple of years now Hagen Shields has managed to keep that murderin' son of his under control. Cam was scared of Hagen. He isn't scared of anyone now. There's no way to stop him. He'll murder for fun, like he did this mornin'."

Dr. Pendexter said surprisingly, "I think you're right. When he backed out of that door, I thought he'd shoot me before he closed it. But still, a doctor's life depends on how he keeps secrets like that, Woodring."

"You won't tell me?"

Doc looked at him a long time, then went over to his desk and sat down. He made a church steeple of his fingers and looked over his glasses at Tip. "A wound above the hip," he began, "can be a very queer thing, Woodring. I've seen some strange cases of hemorrhage in such instances. I've seen a man stagger into a doctor's office with a wound there and he wasn't bleeding at all. But the minute the wound was cleaned, even if it wasn't fatal, it started bleeding again. That's when it's dangerous. You'd think a doctor would have sense enough to let well enough alone, but his training is all in the other direction. For instance—"

Tip stood up, smiling thinly. "Thanks, Doc. I'm sorry you can't tell me what I want to know."

"I'm sorry I can't, too," Dr. Pendexter said. He was smiling, too.

Tip picked up the trail of blood outside Doc's door—as Doc had just told him to do without putting it into those very words—and followed it downstairs. On the sill by the bottom step a few drops had been smeared by the heel of a boot. Reading some meaning into these signs,

Tip knew that Cam Shields had stood here peering out into the street, just as he was doing now.

The next smear, Tip saw, was out on the boardwalk. There were two of them, and their general direction was toward the *Inquirer* office across the street. Tip stared at them a moment, hardly believing. Had Cam Shields crossed the street in view of anyone who cared to look at him, knowing he would be shot on sight? A sick man did strange things, though, and Cam was sick.

Tip looked across the street, judged where Cam would come onto the boardwalk, and then faded back in between the buildings. He went up the alley to the edge of town, strolled across the road in the darkness, took the other alley, and went back into the town. He passed the jail without encountering anyone in the alley. Beside the *Inquirer* building there was ample space in which to walk. He had a hard time squeezing past the open stairway that ran up the side of the building, but he made it.

Looking up and down the street, he saw nobody was coming, so he strolled out to the edge of the boardwalk. There was no mark on the boards; the dust of the street had clung to Cam's boots and smothered any sign. Down on his hands and knees, Tip searched the boards for any sign of the blood, but there was none. He was kneeling that way when he looked up, hearing the door of the *Inquirer* office open. Tip dodged back to the corner of the building, climbing the first step of the stairway and flattening himself against the wall.

Jim, the pressman, strolled by, stopped, walked out to the edge of the boardwalk, lighted a cigar, looked up and down the street, and then went on.

Tip was just ready to step down when his glance fell to the step.

There was the blood spot in the shape of a heel on the lower step!

For one second Tip stared at it, and then it came to him. Lynn's room, of course! These steps led up there, and Cam Shields, sick and hurt, had fled there because it was the only place he knew in town where he could hide. It didn't matter about Anna Bolling being there, for he could threaten her; and he didn't know about Ball. Doc had watched him go, too.

Tip took the steps softly, two at a time, his gun in his hand now. Achieving the top step and the platform, he listened. There was neither light nor sound in there. Gently he tried the doorknob. The catch gave way a little, and Tip's pulse hammered. The door wasn't locked. He pushed, and then the door stopped moving. It was bolted from the inside, not locked from the outside. That was all he needed.

CHAPTER
13

TIP RAISED HIS FOOT and kicked savagely, wheeling his body to one side.

The door crashed open, and on the heel of it came a shot. Tip lunged into the room, sprawling on his face, shooting in the direction of the gun flame. An answering shot hammered out in that close room, and then Tip heard the pounding of heavy boots.

"Anna!" Tip called, coming to his feet.

"He's there, Tip!" Anna's voice came from the corner of the room.

Tip lunged into the dark corridor to the kitchen, and then he heard Cam Shields yelling at the top of his voice, "Here's Tip Woodring! Here's Woodring! Help! Help! Woodring!"

It came from the door beside him. Tip lunged against the door and it was locked. He kicked at it, and Cam shot from the other side of the door. Tip kicked again and again, and the door flew open with a crash. He could make out Cam's figure half out the window. Tip swung up his gun, but before he could fire, a shot came from low in the corner of the room. Cam screamed. Tip saw him grab his chest with the hand that had been holding the window. Then Tip opened up. He sent three shots at Cam, driving him out the window. Cam screamed again, and Tip heard a muffled thud as his body struck the ground below.

"Tip," Ball whispered.

Tip went over to the bed, fumbling for a match. He struck it just as Anna came running in. Ball, his mustaches unbrushed and jet-black against his wan face, was lying in bed grinning. A gun was in his hand, and his other arm was in a sling.

"It took an almighty long time to sight that gun left-handed," Ball said hoarsely.

"Tip, they're coming!" Anna cried.

Tip wheeled and ran for the stair door. There was a blocky figure standing in it, and Tip shot blindly. He saw the man stagger, and Tip ran for him, hearing the pounding of the feet on the stairway outside. These were Bolling's gunnies, ready and primed for him. He caught the man before he fell and then heaved him down the stairway. He caromed into a man coming up, and they both went down, taking two others with them. Out on the street, somebody was shooting, and Tip dodged inside, slamming the door behind him and locking it. He went to the front windows and lifted up the curtain. The street was already alive with men running toward the stairway. He heard one man yell, "Surround the building!" and recognized Jeff Bolling's voice.

He wheeled to Anna. "Don't let them get Ball!" he said. "Load his gun!"

"Where are you going, Tip?"

"Out of here," Tip said.

He ran back through the kitchen and looked out the window. Below, in the alley, he could see a half-dozen men. That way was out, even if he could jump. He went into Lynn's room. The roof of the adjoining building was swarming with men, now. He raced across to Ball's room. Two men were on the roof of the building on that side. Slowly, he let the curtain fall again.

"They out there?" Ball asked.

Tip nodded.

"Give up, son," Ball said. "If they take you alive, you may be able to break that jail."

"Nobody's takin' me anywhere," Tip said thickly. "I got in this jam and I'll get out of it." He went back to the front room and lifted the curtains again. The crowd in the street had thinned out now, scattering around the building.

Tip opened the door and peered out. Three men were waiting down there, guarding the stairs, while on the next roof, two more men were bellied down, pouring a fire into the window of Lynn's room.

Tip went back in the room, told Anna to stand out of the way, then picked up a rocking chair and hurled it through the window. He ran out the door then, and started down the stairs. The guard out in the open had turned to look at the chair that crashed into the street, and Tip was halfway down the stairs before he looked up at the stairs. Tip shot then, and saw the man go down. But the other guard poked his head and arm around the corner and started shooting.

Suddenly, from in between two buildings across the street, a strange six-gun took up the chorus. The guard who had been shooting staggered out into the open, tripped, and fell.

From across the street Buck's voice yelled, "Watch out, Tip! Get over here if you can!"

Tip hit the bottom step, jumped the boardwalk, and rolled under the tie rail, came to his feet and ran. A dozen guns from the roofs of both buildings opened up then. Buck came out from between the buildings, both guns blazing at the men on the roof. Tip ran, and with a haste that would not let him dodge. Slugs from the guns on the roofs in back of him kicked up dust in front of him and to the side of him. He lunged under the tie rail, tripped on the sidewalk, and got up again, making for the black wedge between the two buildings.

And then he saw Buck half turn and go down on the boardwalk.

Tip lunged for him, grabbed his collar, and yanked him into the darkness.

Once there, Tip stopped, and Buck said, "The horses are back there, Tip. Go on!"

"You hit?"

"No. Go on."

Tip said grimly, "You're hit." He leaned down, picked

up Buck's heavy body, and slung it over his shoulder, grunting under the strain. Already men were running across the street. He could hear their slugs drumming into the building fronts as he staggered back to the alley. Tip slung Buck across the horse in front of the saddle, then swung up behind him and roweled his horse. "Put a hand in that stirrup, Buck, and brace yourself."

He streaked down the alley and across the street for the other alley mouth, just as the first man rounding the corner saw him and shot wide. They passed behind the feed stable, took the corner out into the main street, and Tip looked behind. The first riders, two blocks back, were just getting their horses.

Tip knew that a chase as unequal as this would result in only one thing, and that was capture. From here to the canyon mouth it was a straight speed race, and with Buck across his saddle he couldn't hope to win.

"Buck," he said. There was no answer. Tip's belly went cold with fear. At the graveyard he dismounted and lifted Buck off. The pain of the moving roused Buck.

"I got to get them off our trail, Buck," Tip said. "Where you shot?"

"The leg."

"Is it bleedin' bad? Tell the truth!"

"Not very."

Without another word Tip carried him into the graveyard, laid him behind a gravestone, then raced for his horse. His pursuers were past the feed stable now, just leaving the town. Tip swung into the saddle and roweled his horse. His tough little gray stretched out at a long lope, and Tip held him there. Bolling's men and the townsmen with them were shooting blindly in the night. Tip knew that he would have to lead them only slightly till the mouth of the canyon was achieved, and then ride back on the rim as fast as he could, before they wondered at the fleetness of his pony and looked for Buck along the wayside brush.

When he reached the park, he cut straight across it,

barely out of gunshot of the posse. But once he was in the timber, he turned left sharply and urged his horse to its utmost. They skirted the park and came to the rim of the canyon after a long climb in the dark, and then Tip picked his slow way along the lip of the rim back toward the town. It was slow going, for the big boulders here and the rough terrain made for treacherous footing for the horse. Below him, on his left, the rim fell away abruptly to the canyon floor and the road. It seemed hours before he reached the spot where the graveyard should be. He had to guess, for the canyon below was pitch-black.

He stopped, ground-haltered his horse, and then peered down into the canyon. How deep was it? He tried to remember, and had only a vision of its steep sides. He took his lariat and uncoiled it, then found a jut of rock which was substantial enough to hold him and put the loop around it. Then he swung over the rim, and lowered himself, stretching out to touch the ground. But when he came to the end of the rope, his feet were still not touching. He hung there a second, remembering that a lariat is only thirty feet long, and that the cliff looked much higher than that. Then, cold sweat beading his forehead, he dropped. It was a ten-foot drop, and he landed on the moss and thick black dirt of the canyon floor and rolled over.

Coming to his knees and then his feet, he had a feeling of weariness and despair. How was he going to get out of here now? He moved forward and found that he was on the edge of the graveyard.

When he found Buck and shook him, Buck didn't answer. Tip risked a match, and saw that Buck was breathing and that he had bled much. Tip took off his neckerchief and tied it tightly around Buck's leg to stanch the flow of the blood, then looked about him. Bolling's men would soon think of the canyon itself and start beating their way back. They would catch them here helpless, unless Buck could walk. And Buck couldn't, and Tip wasn't going to leave him. He looked off toward the lights of the town, and came to a sudden decision. He picked Buck up, slung him over his shoulder, and started the slow walk to town, listening for the approach of horses.

It took an eternity to reach the edge of town. He did so without being noticed, and then drifted into the shadows at the side of the feed stable. He eased Buck to the ground, paused to drag in great gagging gusts of breath, then went in back of the feed stable. As on his second night here, the hostler was seated in the archway under the lantern, his chair tilted back against the wall.

Tip moved forward toward the doorway, walking quietly. There were several stalled horses feeding now, and their noise covered his. But when he came to the corner of the office, he was still twenty feet from the hostler. He debated pulling his gun and tying up the man, but then the hostler could help Bolling's crew find him. If he wasn't seen, the hostler would never know the identity of his assailant.

Tip pulled back into the shadows. His foot struck a loose horseshoe and scraped it on the boards. Tip gingerly removed his boot from it, paused, then stooped down and picked it up.

He moved to the office corner again, then took the shoe and pitched it through the archway, beyond the hostler. It clanged on a stone in the street, and the hostler jumped. He stared out into the dark street, then came off his chair and walked out of the doorway and stood looking out into the night.

When he decided to go back to his chair, he got only his head turned when Tip's gun barrel rapped him across the skull. After dragging him back out of sight, Tip swiftly saddled the strongest horse in the stable and led it out into the alley.

He brought Buck round, slung him into the saddle, held him there while he climbed up behind him, and then started north up the alley. He didn't pause at any of the streets, and nobody stopped him. In ten minutes they were out of the town, headed north up canyon. When, a few minutes later, they climbed out of the canyon, Tip swung west into the timber.

He rode as long as he dared, for Buck was as limp as a sack of wheat, and his leg was still bleeding. Tip sought the best shelter he could find in the dark, traveling the dry creek beds. Presently he came to a trickle of water that flowed out from a ground seep by some thick grass. He put Buck down and lighted matches to look around him. The canyon walls here were steep, carved out by the storm waters of many centuries. If a rain came in the mountains during the night, this arroyo would run several feet of water. But Tip took that chance. It was well sheltered from sight by high banks, and there was water.

He washed Buck's leg, gave him his coat, took the slicker from behind the stolen saddle and covered him, put a loaded six-gun by his side, then listened to his breathing. A fever would probably set in, but Buck was strong enough to throw that off. Meanwhile, he had to get some help.

He left Buck there and took up the weary ride to the camp at the line. It was well past midmorning when he rode into the camp from the west having made a great half circle.

Lucy saw him first. She was saddling a horse, but when she saw him she stopped. Lynn was nowhere around.

"Where's Buck?" Lucy asked swiftly.

"Hurt, but not bad. He needs you, Lucy." He looked around the deserted camp. "Where's everybody?"

"Bolling's men came and took Pate this morning," Lucy said, her words spare. "Lynn went with them, so they wouldn't shoot him as soon as they were out of sight of the camp."

Tip looked bleakly at her and then rubbed a hand over his face. He was so tired, this news made scarcely an impression on him. "Took Pate?" he echoed dully. "What for?"

"To get you, Tip. You see, they told me about your killing Cam and about getting away. They said they'd killed Buck and they'd get you when you came for Pate." Suddenly Lucy turned away and started to sob. They were great choking sobs, coming from a heart too filled with grief.

Tip stepped down and took her in his arms and stroked her hair, and she cried on his shoulder.

"They can talk, Lucy, but it's just words," Tip said softly. "I'll get Pate, all right—and they won't get me, either. Now, hush, girl."

"Tip, isn't there any end to this?"

"Yes," Tip said softly. "It's in sight."

"But where is it? How will it ever come out?"

Tip smiled wearily over her head. "I don't know, Lucy. I know one thing, though. We'll fight 'em till our back's to the wall, and then we'll fight 'em through the wall if we have to. That's all."

CHAPTER
14

WHEN JOERNS SAW THE TWO GIRLS, Anna Bolling and Lynn Stevens, standing at the door of his office, he rose hurriedly and made a vague gesture with his hands. "Come in."

Lynn walked straight up to his desk and said quietly, "Sit down, Mr. Joerns."

Joerns sat down slowly, his face reflecting his uneasiness. Lynn leaned both hands on the desk and said, "That crew of murderers who have the law in their hands in this town came out and got Pate Shields last night. He's in jail now."

"Uh—did they?" Joerns said.

"They did," Lynn said. "He was over the county line, Mr. Joerns. What have you got to say about that?"

"How do you know he was?"

"I was there and saw them do it. I came into town with them, so they wouldn't shoot Pate!"

Joerns plucked at his lower lip. "Uh—what reason did they give for taking him?"

"They want to use him for bait, so Tip Woodring will come into town again and try to break him out."

"What do you want me to do?" Joerns asked.

"Do?" Lynn blazed. "You took the law in your hands yesterday and made the Shieldses move out of the county! Take it in your hands again and go over there and tell them to free Pate!"

Joerns's face showed distaste. "I haven't the authority."

"You find it!" Lynn blazed. She spoke in a low, level voice. "Mr. Joerns, I haven't shot a gun much. But if you don't get Pate out of that jail, I'm going to wait for you on a dark street and shoot you!"

Joerns's jaw sagged open. "My dear girl—" he began.

"Don't 'my dear girl' me!" Lynn cried. "*Do* something!"

Joerns, his face red, rose, took his hat from the hook,

and went out. Lynn and Anna followed him. They went over to the sheriff's office.

Jeff Bolling was shouting up the stairs to Murray Seth as they entered, and he turned to confront them. His face was haggard, mean-looking, and he hadn't shaved for several days. He scowled at the sight of Joerns with the two girls.

"Jeff," Joerns said, "I understand you have Pate Shields up there in a cell."

"That's right," Bolling said, looking at Lynn. He smiled faintly, insolently.

"What for?" Joerns said.

"She told you, didn't she?"

"Yes. Still, it's illegal. As long as he wasn't in the county you haven't any right to seize him."

Jeff put a foot on a chair and folded his arms on his knee. "Nobody had a right to kill my old man in jail, Joerns. Nobody had a right to burn down our spread. Still, it was done."

"You can't do it, Jeff!" Anna said hotly.

Jeff didn't even look at her. He was looking at Joerns. "And you didn't have a right to force Buck Shields to sell the Bridle Bit, Joerns. Still, you did it."

Joerns flushed and contrived a weak smile. "These girls seem afraid that something will happen to Pate while he's in jail."

Jeff looked at Lynn and sneered. "He'll be safer here than outside, where every bounty hunter in the county will be takin' pot shots at him."

Anna walked up to Jeff and said in a low voice, "Jeff, I've never asked you for much. But I do now. Let Pate go."

Jeff came erect, his eyes flashing. "Sis, unless you get out of here and shut your mouth, I'll do a little talking on my own hook."

Anna paled, Lynn noticed, and then turned away.

Joerns said to Lynn, "I've done my best, Miss Stevens."

Lynn came up to Jeff. "Let's hear you promise, Jeff, that nothing will happen to Pate."

"Nothing will happen," Jeff said nastily, "except he'll get three good meals a day and a lot of sleep. He'll be let out of here as soon as we have Woodring."

Lynn laughed, and it was touched with hysteria. "You get Tip Woodring? That's funny, Jeff. He'll break Pate out of this jail and you'll never know it, because you'll be dead when it happens if you try to stop him."

Jeff grinned wolfishly. "That's the way to talk. Maybe you'll send him."

"Maybe I will!" Lynn said hotly. She had completely lost her temper now and she was talking foolishly, and what's more she didn't care.

Jeff laughed aloud now. "That's a bargain. Now, Joerns, take your beauties out of here before they blow up and spatter all over the ceiling."

Lynn and Anna went out, and Joerns went back to the bank. Up in their rooms again, Lynn sank into a chair and buried her face in her hands. She was so angry she was sick, and her own helplessness made her want to scream and yell. It couldn't go on this way. It just couldn't! Suddenly she laughed, and Anna, who had been watching her, put a hand on her shoulder. "Jeff isn't all bad, Lynn. I don't think he'll hurt Pate."

Lynn leaned back in her chair and closed her eyes. "I wish I believed that, Anna. Anything can happen in this fight—anything."

Anna went to the window and stared moodily down into the street. She gingerly fingered the torn shards of glass where Tip had thrown the chair through the window last night. She turned and looked at Lynn, then said quietly, "Do you think they got away, Lynn?"

"Of course they did."

"But—there was blood out there on the walk across the street. I saw it."

"They're both tough," Lynn said. She opened her eyes and looked at Anna. Before Anna could turn her head, Lynn saw the sadness and tragedy in her face. She said gently, "Buck's all right, Anna."

"But I saw Tip pick him up and carry him away!" Anna cried in a choked voice. She held her fists tightly clenched for a few seconds, then relaxed. "I'm not going to be afraid," she said in a firm voice. "I've stood worse than this, and I can again."

Lynn came over and took her arm and turned her around and looked in her eyes. "You've just got to believe it will come out all right, Anna. It's a funny kind of faith to have in a man, but it works. I know. Just keep *knowing* nothing will happen to them, and it won't."

She turned around then and said in a flat voice, "I'm going to sleep," and went into her room and closed the door. Anna went in to see Ball and talked with him awhile, afterward going out into the kitchen.

A knock on the door brought her into the front room. She opened the door to confront Murray Seth. Strangely enough, he was shaved and had on a clean shirt. Anna said, "Hello, Murray. What do you want?" and didn't move out of the door.

Murray said, "I want to talk to you."

"All right, go ahead."

"No. Inside, where we can sit down."

Anna sighed and stepped aside, and Murray shuffled into the room. He saw the window and shook his head somberly. "That damn Indian can wreck a place quicker than any ten men I ever knowed."

"He'll do the same to you."

Murray chuckled. "No, he won't. He's got to back-water, now. Last night took a little of the sand out of his craw, I reckon."

"They got away, didn't they?"

"But they was shot up," Murray said in a matter-of-fact voice. "There was blood across the street and out by the graveyard, where one of 'em left the hurt one and sucked us all down the canyon. There was blood on that gray up on the rimrock, too."

Anna said in a small voice, "Which one was it, do you think?"

"Hurt? Why, Buck Shields, I figure. I'll tell you why. Nobody but that damn Tip Woodring would have had the nerve to leave a man there in the graveyard and then come back for him. Buck would of done it, only I misdoubt if he'd of thought of it."

Anna turned away and sat down, fighting to keep control of herself. She wanted to ask one more question and didn't dare. She sat there, staring at her hands. Murray pulled a chair over close to her and sat down.

"That's what I wanted to talk about," Murray said, hunching his chair closer. "Now that Buck's either dead or goin' to die, it makes it pretty easy for us."

Anna looked up at him, speechless. There was a horror in her eyes that Murray Seth in his fatuousness did not even recognize. He even took hold of her hand.

"You been pretty stubborn, Anna, but I think it's about time you give in," Murray said tolerantly. "I've asked Jeff, and he says it's all right with him. You and me could buy that Shields place when it comes up for auction in a couple days, and it would give us a right nice setup."

Anna withdrew her hand and slapped Murray viciously across the face. He took it unsmilingly and didn't move off the chair, only stared at her. "The reason I think you'll do it," he said carefully, "is because if you don't I aim to tell what I know about Blackie Mayfell's murder and your part in it."

Something happened to Anna. She came off her chair fighting, clawing at Murray's face and kicking and sobbing wildly. Murray laughed, and gathered her in his big arms and tried to kiss her.

Suddenly Lynn's voice rapped out, "Let her go, Murray!"

Murray looked over in the direction of the kitchen. Lynn Mayfell, in a gray wrap held together by one hand, had a gun leveled at him, and there was murder in her eyes.

Murray took his hands off Anna, who was crying, and stepped back.

"If you think you can make that door before I can shoot, Murray, you better try it. I can't hit a man running as well as I can hit him standing still."

She cocked the gun, and it wobbled as she stretched for the hammer. For once, Murray Seth thought fast. He lunged for the door, and Lynn shot. It was a wild shot, knocking a sliver of wood out of the floor behind Murray, but it sufficed. He slammed the door open, lunged down the stairs, tripped, and rolled the rest of the way. Hitting the boardwalk, he scrambled to his feet and ran for shelter.

Lynn let the gun sag and came over to Anna, who was still crying. Lynn took her in her arms.

"I've had enough, Lynn," Anna whispered. "I'm going."

"But you can't, child. There's no place to go."

"I'm going to find Buck. I've *got* to!"

"But how?"

"I—I can track, Lynn. Look, won't Tip come to get Lucy there at the line and won't she go to Buck? Oh, I know I can find him, Lynn! I've got to!"

Lynn hugged her to her. "All right, Anna. It's better than waiting this way, not knowing how he is or where he is. You can try."

She wanted desperately to ask Anna the meaning of the threat Murray Seth had made that he would disclose Anna's part in Blackie Mayfell's murder. But she couldn't now, she just couldn't.

She watched Anna change into her riding-clothes and walked down to the feed stable with her and watched her pick out a horse, certain that it was futile and wishing it weren't.

Anna came to the abandoned camp at the county line in midafternoon. The Shieldses' wagon was still there and so was the tarp, but the bedding was gone, which meant Lucy was gone. Out of all the tracks that scarred the camp site Anna knew she must pick those of Tip's horse, a horse she was not familiar with.

For a moment she pondered this problem amid the con-

fusion of tracks. Logically, the tracks of Tip's horse would
be the freshest, since he had ridden into camp to get Lucy.
But how many hours ago was that, she wondered. Even an
Indian would shrug at this impossible chore. Then it oc-
curred to her that she knew the tracks of Lucy's horse and
that Lucy would be riding with Tip. Accordingly, starting
from the trampled-down spot where the rope corral had
been, she picked up what looked to be the most recent
tracks of Lucy's mount. Her first lead was a wrong one, for
those tracks soon merged with those of a smaller horse
which, of course, would be Pate's. Doubtless Lucy and Pate
had gone out together to drag in wood.

Patiently she returned to the corral and tried again.
This time the tracks of Lucy's horse took her over to where
the bedrolls had lain. Then they took off into the timber
and were soon joined by another set of tracks. These were
of a big horse; they were not only large but were pressed
deeply into the fresh earth. Time and again as she followed
them they obliterated older tracks, and Anna felt a quiet
exultation. These must be the tracks that Lucy's and Tip's
horses made on their departure.

By that time it was close to dark. She ate part of the
lunch she had brought with her, then crawled into the
wagon, wrapped herself in the tarp, and went to sleep.

She was up at daylight, knowing she was facing a task
that was almost insurmountable. Tip, to make sure that
Bolling's men would not follow his tracks from the camp,
was certain to use all the skill at his command to cover
his tracks on the way back to Buck. Only one thing was in
her favor; Tip would be in such a hurry to get back to
Buck that he would be careless. But not very careless, Anna
knew.

Two miles from camp, she lost Tip's tracks in a stretch
of malpais, and that was only the beginning. By noon, she
had found them again; they had come out by some brush
not fifteen feet from where they went in. By nightfall,
Anna had succeeded in tracking Tip a bare five miles from
camp. She went to bed that night hungry, and with a

wholesome respect for Tip Woodring's ability.

Next day, she was to meet worse. She got three miles behind her by late afternoon, and then the tracks disappeared in a stream. She was faint from hunger and weariness, and a feeling of despair settled on her as darkness fell. It would take her two weeks to find Buck this way, and she had neither the food nor the strength nor the ability to go on.

She built a fire and ate the last of her food, and then pondered what she was to do. She decided, after much thought, that she would build up a big fire, and shoot her gun. If Tip was within hearing-distance, he would come. If he wasn't, nothing was lost that wasn't lost already.

Dragging big logs onto her fire, she started firing her shots in groups of three, the universal frontier call for help. But at midnight, both her shells and her wood were used up, and nobody had come in answer. She took the piece of tarp she had cut for a blanket, rolled up in it, and cried herself to sleep.

Sometime in the night she was wakened by a hand on her shoulder. She opened her eyes to see a man's head and Stetson framed against the sky.

"Anna?" It was Tip's voice.

"Oh, Tip. You came! How is Buck?"

"He's plenty sick, but he'll pull through the fever all right."

"Take me to him, Tip. Quick!"

"You better rest."

"I've had my rest." She threw the tarp off her. "You wait here till I catch my pony."

"He's caught and saddled," Tip said, chuckling. "I figured you'd be in a hurry."

They rode north again, and presently left the cedars for the timbered country and later came to the camp.

There was a small fire on the grass, and Lucy was kneeling over Buck. She turned to greet them and she was smiling, her face radiant. "The fever broke, Tip! He can talk to me!" She smiled at Anna, too.

Anna walked slowly to where Buck lay and looked down at him. Buck grinned weakly at her and tiredly raised a hand in salute.

Anna dropped to her knees beside him and took his hand. Tip touched Lucy on the shoulder and when she turned to look at him, beckoned her away.

Anna didn't speak for a long while, holding Buck's hand. Finally she said, "You look awful, Buck. Were you pretty sick?"

Buck grinned and whispered irrelevantly, "You're what I've been dreamin' about for four months these last three nights."

Anna didn't say anything, and Buck went on in a whisper. "I kept wantin' to die and end this and you kept sayin' to me, 'Don't do it, Buck. We've still got a chance.'"

With a soft cry Anna leaned over and kissed him and hugged his head to her breast. "Oh, Buck, nothing matters any more. I don't care what you've done or what you've been, just so I can be with you!"

Buck said gravely, "And I don't care what you've done, Anna. Nobody needs to know you killed him. It was— It just had to be, I reckon."

Anna looked down at him. "Killed who?" she asked in a tight voice.

"Blackie Mayfell."

"But you did it, Buck, didn't you?" Anna asked.

Buck slowly raised himself up on one arm and stared at her. "No. I thought you did."

Anna cried out with delight, and then held him.

Afterward, she called to Tip and Lucy, and they came over. Buck was grinning from ear to ear, and he had a firm clasp on Anna's hand.

"Tip," Anna said, "you remember one night in town you asked me questions I wouldn't answer? I will now."

Tip looked from her to Buck and back to her again.

"You see," Anna said, "Buck and I have loved each other for a long time. But we knew that we'd never know peace until this fight was over. I—" she looked at Buck—

"I guess we both were fools enough to think we owed loyalty to our own. Well, the last time we met, Blackie Mayfell, that big prospector, saw us together. We were sitting beside our horses in one of the canyons on our range, and he came around the bend, driving his burros. He knew us, and he knew our families."

"And we ran," Buck said grimly. "But we knew he saw us."

"Buck was angry and so was I," Anna said, "and we were both afraid of what might happen."

"I was afraid of what Ben Bolling would do to her when he found out," Buck said grimly.

"Two days later," Anna went on, "I found Blackie Mayfell dead. I—I thought Buck had killed him, trying to protect me. I didn't touch him and I didn't tell anyone. Then Jeff found Mayfell and saw my tracks and thought I'd killed him. He and Dad talked it over with me and I denied ever having been there. I was a fool," Anna said bitterly, "but I was afraid to admit any of it, for fear they would find out about me and Buck. They took his body and dumped it on Bridle Bit land."

"The rest I've told you about," Buck said to Tip. "I backtracked and saw Anna's tracks, and then I thought she'd killed Mayfell to keep him from going to her father."

Anna looked eagerly at Tip, and Buck regarded him silently.

"Each of you thought the other did it," Tip said quietly, "and now you find you didn't and you don't know who did kill him." He smiled wryly, and came to his feet. He stared at the fire a long time, then shook his head. "Lynn," he said quietly, "is Blackie's daughter. That leaves her just where she's always been. Nowhere." He laughed shortly, looking at them.

"And you, too, doesn't it, Tip?" Anna said gently.

"Yeah, and me, too," Tip said absently, almost as an afterthought. Lucy remembered that.

CHAPTER
15

THE AUCTION WAS TO BE HELD in the Masonic Hall above Sig's Neutral Elite, and the hour was set for ten. At a quarter to ten the hall was jammed, but in the front row of benches and in the corner Lynn had found a seat. Buck and Tip would want to know who bought the Bridle Bit and what they had paid for it. If it hadn't been for that, she wouldn't have come, for the idea of watching what Buck and Lucy had risked their lives for being split up and sold to the highest bidder made Lynn a little sick.

Joerns was behind the table on the platform, and he called the meeting to order.

"I haven't had handbills printed," Joerns began, "because it wasn't worth it. None of the movable property on the Bridle Bit is for sale, only the buildings—a seven-room house, a wagon shed, a blacksmith shop, the corrals, and the land. Can you remember that?"

There was a murmur of assent, and Joerns went on in a businesslike, unemotional voice that galled Lynn. She shifted in her seat and listened dully to the recitation.

"The land is fifteen hundred acres, mostly in timber. The boundaries are posted on the back wall of this room. I might add that the western boundary adjoins several hundred thousand acres of open range, semidesert and desert. The Bridle Bit is amply watered and sheltered and the title"—he paused and looked belligerently around him —"is clear. It is guaranteed by this bank. One more thing. Anyone buying this place, unless his name is Shields, is assured of good neighbors with peaceful intentions." He paused. "All right, who will open the bid?"

"Five thousand," a voice said. The bid was kicked up to seven thousand five hundred, the offer coming from Murray Seth.

"Seven thousand five hundred," Joerns said, adding, "This is cash, you understand."

"That's what I'm givin'," Seth growled.

"Do I hear a higher bid?" Joerns asked, raising his gavel.

"Ten thousand."

In a murmur of talk, everyone, including Lynn, tried to see who the bidder was. He sat against the wall on the second bench, a man almost in middle age, lean, with a long wedge of pale face topped by graying hair. His face was dissolutely handsome, and his clothes were an elegant black.

"I'm bid ten thousand," Joerns said halfheartedly over the talk, then cracked his gavel and repeated the offer in the ensuing silence.

"Eleven thousand," Murray Seth said sourly.

"Twelve," the man in black said.

"Twelve thousand one hundred," Murray said.

"Thirteen thousand."

Joerns repeated the offer, and Murray Seth said, "Wait a minute, Joerns." He turned to Jeff Bolling beside him and whispered something, and Bolling nodded.

"Thirteen thousand one hundred," Seth said.

"Fourteen thousand," came the lazy, drawling voice.

A babble of talk stopped the proceedings for a moment, while Joerns hammered futilely on the table. When order was restored, he repeated the bid. Suddenly the man in black stood up and raised his long-fingered, well-kept hands in good-natured protest.

"Gentlemen," he said amiably, and looked at Seth, who was glaring at him. "I am not a cattleman, and do not intend to ranch this piece of property. I am looking for a place to rest, a home, a mountain home, and the Shields place has taken my fancy. If my opponent"—here he bowed to Murray Seth—"wants to lease all but a few acres from me, or even buy it from me, I am willing to sell."

He paused, and Murray said nothing. "But I am determined to have the house and the park. If my opponent still wants to argue, let's double the price already bid and get down to business." He looked at Murray and smiled faintly.

Jeff Bolling said curiously, "You ain't an agent for the Shieldses, are you, mister?"

The man in black turned his hands palms up. "I don't know a Shields, I never saw a Shields, and, unless I've been grossly misled, I don't ever want to see a Shields."

That brought a laugh from the crowd, and Lynn bit her lip in anger. Whoever this man was, he understood the dramatic gesture, the right word, the winning affability, and the infectious smile of a born persuader. These people liked him already, Lynn could tell. And she didn't.

"That's a funny way to buy a ranch," Murray Seth growled.

"Every man is entitled to his own eccentricity," the man in black pointed out. "Yours is cattle. Mine is wanting a pleasant home in this pleasant place."

He looked at Joerns. "All right, Mr. Auctioneer. Proceed."

"Fourteen thousand," Joerns said weakly. He stared at the man in black. "You understand the terms?"

"I have the cash with me," the man replied.

Everyone looked at Murray Seth. He stood up and said, "Hell, ain't no sense in biddin' for a place I can lease or buy."

"And for a lot less than you've already bid," the man in black said. He laughed and came over and shook hands with Murray and then with Jeff Bolling. They followed him up to the table, where Joerns had the deed.

Lynn hung back while the man in black counted out the money and received the deed. When he was finished, Joerns put out his hand. "Might as well know each other, since we're neighbors now. My name's Joerns."

"A pleasure, Mr. Joerns," the man in black said.

"I didn't get the name," Joerns said.

"It doesn't matter, gentlemen. I'm only an agent." He turned to the crowd and said, "I owe you a drink for that deception. Let's go downstairs."

Lynn went out with the crowd and headed for her rooms. She didn't even know the name of the man who had bought the Bridle Bit, and apparently, he wasn't going to tell it.

She walked back to her rooms, feeling discouraged. The fate of the Bridle Bit was signed and sealed, with Tip on the dodge, Buck dead or hurt, Pate in jail, and Jeff Bolling already friends with the new owner.

She opened the door and found Anna standing there.

"Hello, Lynn Mayfell," Anna said, smiling. She laughed at the look of dismay on Lynn's face, then pulled her into a chair and told her of finding Buck, and of the reason that she had hidden what she knew of Blackie Mayfell's death.

Lynn listened with a sinking heart. In the back of her mind she had always believed that Anna, if she would talk, held the key to her father's death. And now she knew that Anna had never known. They were farther away from the truth than they had ever been. All these months had been wasted and lost. Anna understood a little of this, but not all of it.

"What did Tip say when you told him?" Lynn asked.

Anna laughed ruefully. "He acted just like you're acting now."

Lynn smiled faintly. "It doesn't give us a chance to be very happy that you and Buck are clear." She kissed Anna and went in to see Ball, and then went into her room. Sitting on the bed, she stared out the window. Everything was flat and dull and tasteless, and the drive had gone out of her. She was too dispirited to feel bad. Suddenly she thought of Tip and wanted to be with him. The feeling was overpowering, and she didn't try to master it. She went out and said to Anna, "I'm going to see—Buck. Will you stay here tonight?"

"I'll stay anywhere anytime," Anna said happily. Then her face clouded. "You must be careful about covering your tracks."

"I'll be careful," Lynn said and smiled wryly. "I've cov-

ered them for you and Buck for several months, haven't
I?"

They both laughed, but Lynn's laugh was only half-
hearted. She wondered as she put on her riding-clothes if
she would ever laugh again.

CHAPTER
16

LYNN WAS CAREFUL about leaving town. She went up the canyon, and turned in the opposite direction from where Buck was hidden. Then she pulled off the trail, circled, and went back and watched the canyon. She watched it for an hour, waiting to see if anybody would follow her, but nobody did.

Afterward, she crossed the canyon, climbed into the timber again, and headed down toward the place Anna had described.

It was dark when she saw the campfire, and only seconds after she saw it Tip challenged her from the dark. "Who is it?"

"Lynn, Tip."

"Oh." Tip rode up to her and put his horse beside hers. "How's Buck?"

"Doin' fine," Tip said lifelessly.

Lynn, on a sudden impulse, said, "Oh, Tip, I know how you feel. Anna told me about it."

"I don't feel a tenth as bad as you do," Tip growled. "I'm just—well, lost is the word for it."

"I know."

"Sure you do," Tip said, and added vehemently, "It isn't the money, Lynn. Hell, I'd pay ten thousand if I had it to help you with this!"

"Don't talk about it," Lynn said. "Don't let Buck know how I feel."

They entered the circle of firelight and dismounted. Lucy was sitting by Buck, and Lynn went straight to him. He seemed cheerful, but he scanned Lynn's face anxiously. When Lynn sat down beside him, Buck said, "This is kind of a funeral for you, ain't it, Lynn?"

"A little bit."

Buck looked over at Tip, who was squatted near the fire warming his hands. "Me and Anna are the only ones that've come out of this without grief."

"Don't be too sure of that, Buck," Lynn said.

Buck said quickly, "Has anything happened to Anna?"

"No, I didn't mean that. But Anna is homeless, and so are you, Buck. That's not much to be happy about."

"She's enough to be happy about," Buck said quietly.

Lynn said idly, "They sold the Bridle Bit at auction today."

Buck looked interested. "To Bolling?"

"No. Murray Seth bid on it, but a stranger beat him out."

Buck asked the price paid, and Lynn told him, and he lapsed into silence. Lynn described the queer arrangement agreed upon, that Murray Seth could have the graze if the house was left to the stranger. Tip raised his head at this bit of information and came over and sat down beside Lynn.

"That's a funny setup," he remarked. "Who was it, some remittance man from the East?"

"No, he wasn't an easterner."

"What was his name?" Buck asked.

"That was funny. He wouldn't give it. Said he was acting as an agent for somebody, and admitted, after the deal was cinched, that he'd lied about being taken by the beauty of the place."

Tip scowled. "Lied, hunh? Did he lie to Seth about leasing the graze?"

"No. That stood."

Tip looked over at Buck, puzzled. "Then what does he want the place for if he isn't going to live on it and leases out the rest of the land, except the prairie, to Seth?"

"I don't know," Lynn said.

"What did he look like?" Buck asked. "An old-timer?"

Lynn said thoughtfully, "No, he had grayish hair and looked about forty-five. He had a long face and a very friendly manner, and he wore black clothes. He looked like a gambler, maybe."

Lynn was suddenly aware that Tip was staring at her with an intent, waiting expression. His face had tautened expectantly.

"Why, Tip, what's—"

"Describe him again," Tip said in a low voice, a strange voice.

Lynn did, trying to remember everything about the stranger, and Tip hung on her every word. When she had finished, he said hoarsely, "He had long thin hands, a card dealer's hands, didn't he? He had a habit of puttin' his hands on his hips, didn't he? He wore a black suit and a black vest with a little edge of black silk. He had—"

"Yes, yes!" Lynn said excitedly. "Tip, do you know him?"

Tip said hoarsely, "So will you, Lynn. That's *Rig Holman!*"

He stood up, looking at the fire, his thoughts racing, his face pale and excited. Lynn came to her feet and said, "Tip," and Tip motioned her to silence. It was as if he were waiting for something to explode. He reached out and took Lynn's elbow, still staring at the fire, and his grip made Lynn want to cry out. When he turned to Lynn, there was something in his face that she had never seen before, and his eyes looked like burning coals.

"Lynn," he said softly, hoarsely, *"that's the man who killed your father!"*

Lynn didn't answer for a moment, because she couldn't. Then she cried, "How do you know, Tip?"

"You never saw Rig Holman?"

"No. He sent a messenger with a bank draft to give me my money."

Tip said swiftly, the words tumbling out, his grip getting tighter on her arm, "Lynn, I've been a damned, blind fool! Who else could it be but Rig? It wasn't Buck, it wasn't Anna, it wasn't any of the Shieldses or any of the Bollings. They didn't have any reason. The reason was gold—and it was there before me all the time!"

"But I don't—"

"Yes, you do," Tip said, his words riding her down. "Who besides you knew what Blackie was after? Only Rig! And now Rig turns up to buy that prairie on Buck's place." He wheeled to Buck. "Did Blackie ever prospect on that part, Buck?"

"Sure. But he prospected everywhere."

Tip looked at Lynn. "There's your answer! Blackie Mayfell's gold is under the grass of that prairie, Lynn. Blackie went back into this country where the Shieldses and the Bollings were feudin', and he knew he might be caught up in the fight and killed. So he had Rig Holman insure him, and like a fool he told Rig about the gold. But there was no way Rig could get the gold, after he followed Blackie over here and killed him. Hagen Shields wouldn't sell out. Hagen was there till he died. So he sent me over to do it for him! His payoff to you, Lynn, would throw off all suspicion!"

Lynn tried to speak again, but the fire that was in Tip's eyes scared her.

"He knew I'd land in this fight. He knew I'd be dragged into it. And he figured I was wild enough to clean out the Shieldses and the Bollings for him, so he could step in and buy." He cursed wickedly with pointed fury. "He could kill Blackie easy because Blackie wouldn't suspect him. Then he toted Blackie's body as far from the real site of the gold as he could."

He laughed suddenly, unpleasantly. "Well, I was his man, all right. I came in here and broke up the fight and downed the Shieldses, and he stepped in and got the place. I busted this feud for him, *but it's not finished yet!*"

"Tip," Buck warned, seeing the signs.

Tip whirled and ran for his horse. Lynn ran after him, and caught his arm just as he was swinging into the saddle. "Tip, what are you going to do?"

"I'm goin' to cut loose the dogs," Tip said, his voice surprisingly mild. "They may be hell's own kin in that town, but they'll be damn sick cousins in a little while."

"Tip, you can't go in there! They're waiting for you! They know you'll be in!" Lynn cried.

"Sure they do," Tip said and laughed.

"The minute you set foot in there to talk to Rig Holman, Jeff Bolling and his crowd will swarm all over you!"

Tip looked down at her terrified face, and he shook his head slowly. "Lynn, Jeff Bolling won't come after me. Because I'm goin' to rub out his mark before I ever see Rig Holman."

Buck struggled to get up, but he was too weak to make it. "Tip, you can't go in there alone! Dammit, you can't! Wait a few days until I'm on my feet!"

"I'm not waitin' any more. I've waited too long now."

He touched his horse with his spurs and rode out of the circle of firelight. Lucy, who had silently listened to all this, said, "Buck, can't we do something?"

"Go after him!" Buck cried. "Hell, they'll murder him!"

But Lynn was already moving. She stepped into the saddle and pushed out of the firelight after Tip. Lucy stood watching her, and her face was so sad that Buck, still propped up on his elbow, said, "Do you want to go, too, Lucy?"

Lucy smiled at him, and Buck thought it was the most wistful smile he had ever seen. "I want to, Buck, but he'd send me back. And he won't send Lynn."

Buck said gently, "Lucy, look up here."

Lucy did, and she was not far from tears.

"I didn't know it was that way, sis. Does Tip know?"

"He doesn't know, and he never will, Buck, because he's never taken the trouble to look." She walked over and looked down at him. "It's all right, Buck. I knew it was Lynn from the moment I saw them together, and I'm glad. I couldn't help loving him and I'm proud I did, but it was never any use. A man makes his choice a long time before he knows it himself, and Tip Woodring has made his choice. It—it just wasn't me, Buck."

A hundred yards away from the fire Lynn made out Tip's form in the trees and she called to him, and he stopped.

"There's no use tryin' to stop me," Tip said patiently. "I'm goin', Lynn."

"I know you are. So am I."

"You're goin' back!"

"Oh, no, I'm not. This is my fight more than it is yours, Tip Woodring. Blackie Mayfell was my father."

Tip stared wrathfully at her in the dark. He was helpless to make her return and he knew it and he was secretly glad.

"All right," he said finally. "This won't be pretty to watch, but you asked for it."

When they were in sight of town, Lynn put her hand out and caught the bridle of Tip's horse and pulled him up.

"Tip, you've *got* to let me help. There must be something I can do, isn't there?"

"No," Tip said quietly. "Thanks."

"How do you know Rig Holman is still in town?"

"I'll find out."

"That's something I can do," Lynn said. She spurred her horse ahead and called back, "I'll meet you in back of the *Inquirer*, Tip."

Tip didn't try to stop her. He looked ahead at the lights of this town. He had whipped it once, and then it had whipped him, and now he was coming back for the last try. Either he would whip it this time, or he would never know that he hadn't.

He took to the alleys again, but this time he avoided going past the jail. He wasn't quite ready for that yet. Going down the side street he turned at the cross street and came up the alley from the other direction, dismounting in back of the *Inquirer*. He hunkered down against the wall there, feeling no impatience, only a sort of cool wind touching him. He could wait for anything now, because he knew what he was going to do.

Presently he saw Lynn turn into the alley, and he was erect when she stopped and swung out of the saddle.

"He's still there, Tip. His baggage is, anyway."

"Good."

A pause. "How do you plan to go about it, Tip?" She tried to hold her voice steady, forcing the fear out of it.

"I don't plan," Tip said. "I'm just goin' to the jail, that's all."

"Jeff is there, and so is Murray Seth. I saw them when I rode past. So are two other men."

"All right," Tip said. The impatience was here now, the knowledge that he was going to do it being pushed by the desire to be done with it.

He and Lynn faced each other there in the dark.

Lynn said, "Do you think Holman will run when he hears the fight?"

"Let him run. There's nowhere he can hide that I won't find him." He drew out one gun, opened the loading gate, and spun the cylinder. It was loaded. He tried the other, and it was loaded, too. There were only those sounds in the quiet night, and they made Lynn's spine go cold.

"Well," Tip said, "I'll see you later."

Lynn wanted to throw her arms around him, to hold him, to fight him back, and then she wanted to go with him, and she knew all the time that she would do none of these things. She had to let him go, because this was what men lived by. She only said, "Come back, Tip."

But Tip didn't hear her. He walked toward the street between the buildings, squeezed past the stairs, and came to the boardwalk. He paused there a brief moment, scanning the street. The light from the lamp in the sheriff's office lay across the boardwalk in a luminous block. Across the street, the buildings were black blocks in the night. Four horses just beyond the shaft of light from the office moved softly in the dark, their muffled stomping and the jingling of their bits a muted warning sound.

Tip's nerves were keyed up now, as he began his slow walk toward the sheriff's office. He passed a dark store building, and his pace increased and then he came abreast the saddle shop, and then the alley, and now his hands fell to his guns. He could hear Jeff Bolling laugh in the office.

Crack! The flat slam of a rifleshot was simultaneous with the *whup!* of the slug as it buried itself in one of the clapboards of the sheriff's office just beyond Tip's head. Tip lunged into the passageway between the saddle shop and jail, hearing someone come out of the sheriff's chair with a lunge and run for the street, yelling, "Here he is, boys!" It was Jeff Bolling's voice.

Tip moved on toward the window, looked in, and saw the room was deserted. He swung a leg over the sill just as Murray Seth lunged out of the stairway door, heading for the street door. He and Tip saw each other at the same time. Murray, still running, swung his gun up across his body, just as Tip's gun finished its tight arc and exploded twice in rapid succession. The shots drove Murray off balance, and he crashed into the table and went down. Tip was now running for the street door. He lunged over Murray's body and rammed into a man in the doorway. He shot blindly, so close to his body that he felt the scalding burn of the powder, and then he slugged the man out of his way, caroming him into a second man behind him. This man tripped and sat down, and as he was falling he shot wildly. Tip kicked at his face and felt his boot connect and then he fell, rolling in between the feet of the horses at the tie rail. He came up on one knee and lunged out into the road, just as the horses began to plunge and kick.

And then, from his kneeling position, he saw Jeff Bolling standing in the middle of the street, half turned toward him, a gun in each hand. Tip came up slowly just as Jeff shot. It was almost a tentative shot, as if Jeff were trying to make sure of his man. Then, feet planted wide apart, a kind of wild panic took hold of Jeff Bolling. He used his guns as if they were clubs, swinging each down and firing as if the fear that rode him could not push him

fast enough. Tip swung up his gun shoulder-high, then
let it settle and when Jeff Bolling's head and then his chest
hove up through the indistinct sight, he pulled the trigger.

It was as if some invisible hand had brushed Jeff Bolling
down. His feet still planted, his boots in the same tracks
in the dust, he went over backward, and Tip heard the
wind go out of him as he fell. Jeff bent one knee and
dragged his foot back, and then the knee fell sideways,
and his head turned over in the dust, his cheek lying in it
as on a pillow.

Tip looked up beyond Jeff to the porch of Baylor's store.
A half-dozen men, all townsmen, regarded him in silence.

"I'm still deputy sheriff in this town," Tip announced
quietly. "Does anybody want to argue that?"

He stood out there in the street, a dark, shadowy figure,
erect and waiting and inviting a fight, standing straight
as a gun barrel, his free hand fisted, the gun loose in the
other.

The first man on the steps let his gun slide back into its
holster and turned and went back into the store. The
others followed him.

Tip walked down the middle of the street, ramming
fresh loads in his gun. He paused by Jeff Bolling, looking
down at him. Jeff's face, for the first time in his life, was
peaceful-looking and quiet. Tip stepped over him, hit the
boardwalk, and then tramped downstreet toward the hotel. He met three men on the boardwalk, and they knew
him and were warned by his look. They looked upstreet
and saw that figure lying in the road and then they moved
against the building, letting him pass.

He went into the hotel and crossed the lobby and
tramped deliberately up the stairs. As his head came level
with the top step, he could look down the hall and see
Lynn Mayfell, a gun in her small fist, facing an open doorway. Behind and to one side of her, Uncle Dave Shawn,
the bedclothes wrapped around him, had a shotgun
slacked off his shoulder. Lynn didn't turn as she heard
Tip's step.

Tip shouldered between them and against the outside wall of the room, hands over his head, stood Rig Holman, his face a pasty gray.

"Tip!" he cried. Relief flooded his face, and he lowered his hands. Tip stepped into the room and took hold of the door to close it. He felt it stop halfway, and he heard Lynn's voice say, "No. I'm coming in."

Tip didn't look at her. He was watching Rig Holman, watching the confidence flood into his face and fear wash out.

"What in hell is this?" Rig asked curiously. "They've been holdin' me against this wall for five minutes."

"He came in with a rifle, Tip," Lynn said quietly.

Tip smiled then. "Sit down, Rig. I'm sorry you've been bothered."

Rig seated himself onto the bed, looking first at Tip and then at Lynn.

"This is Lynn Mayfell, Rig," Tip murmured. "The girl you paid the money to. Blackie Mayfell's daughter. Remember Blackie?" His voice was soft, gentle, deceptive.

Only Rig's eyes were wary now; the rest of him was relaxed. He regarded Tip closely, and Tip knew he was wondering how much was known.

"Sure I do," Rig said confidently. "I don't understand the welcome with the gun, though." He looked curiously at Lynn, whose back was to the wall, and who still held the six-gun trained on Rig.

Tip sank into the chair and waved a hand carelessly. "Oh, forget that, Rig. Let's talk about other things," Tip said gently, and a wiser man than Rig Holman would have been warned by that gentleness.

Rig's smile flashed. It was the old smile, and now Tip saw that it was as phony as tin money.

"Sure," Rig said. He drew a sack of tobacco from his pocket and rolled a smoke. Tip marveled at how steady his hands were, his gambler's hands.

Rig lighted his smoke and said, "I've been lookin' for you, Tip. I wanted some advice." He laughed suddenly.

"You aren't exactly easy to find these last few days, according to the town."

"Not very," Tip said quietly. "Advice on what?"

"I bought a place today. The Shields place. Know it?"

"I've heard of it. Go on."

"It was up for auction and I picked it up. Fifteen hundred acres. Is it a good buy for fourteen thousand?"

"A very good buy."

Rig looked up at Lynn. She still held the gun on him. He said nervously to Tip, "For God's sake, Tip. Make her put that gun down! What's the matter with her?"

"Nervous, Rig?"

"Why should I be?" Rig said defiantly. There was a little quiver in the cigarette he was holding. "Well, I bought it," Rig said, watching Tip. His confidence was just beginning to crack.

"What for?" Tip asked. "Going to ranch?"

"No, I wanted a place to come to now and then. I like to get away from the tables every once in a while."

"You can get a long way from a gamblin'-table on fifteen hundred acres, Rig. Why so much land?"

"Oh, I only wanted the park up there and the house," Rig said.

He was sweating, Tip saw. Little beads of perspiration were forming on his forehead.

"That's what I wanted to see you about, Tip."

"What?"

"I wondered if you'd go half and half with me on the place. You ranch it, and we'll split whatever it makes." He stared intently at Tip, licking his lips.

Tip understood him. What he was trying to say was, that *if* Tip knew of the gold there, then he was willing to split fifty-fifty with him to keep it a secret. A kind of wicked relish for this scene was having its way with Tip now, and he pretended he hadn't understood.

"Why, Rig, you know I'm ranchin' up in the short-grass country. That is, I will if I can find Blackie's killer and earn that ten thousand."

"Don't bother with that," Rig said sharply. "This is a good ranch. It'll make us money. I'll pay you well, too."

"How much?"

"Why, ten thousand the first year."

Tip drawled quietly, "That's a nice offer, Rig. Mighty handsome."

Rig was puzzled. He wiped his forehead with the sleeve of his coat and for one moment despair showed in his eyes. He couldn't understand Tip's actions. Then he laughed. "Well, I think a lot of you, Tip. I'd like to help you. You don't seem to be doing so well here."

"I'm makin' out," Tip said gently. "You'd be surprised, Rig, how close I am to makin' out pretty well."

Rig swallowed. He shuttled his glance to Lynn, who still held the gun on him, and then back to Tip. Tip's gaze had never left Rig's face.

Rig asked the question then that he knew he was going to have to ask, the question that would be the test. But he wanted to put it off as long as he could. He said, "Makin' out? You haven't got Blackie's killer yet, have you?"

Tip scoured his chin with his hand, regarding Rig with a faint smile. "Not quite yet."

Here it was. Rig stammered, "You—you know who he is?"

"Oh, yes," Tip said quickly. "I know who he is."

"Who?"

There was a long pause. The sweat was streaming off Rig's face, and his hands were shaking so he couldn't stop them.

Tip, his eyes wicked, but a faint smile still on his face, threw a leg over the chair arm and said, "Rig, I come in here for a nice visit with you and then you start talkin' business. It's business, business, business all the time with you. No chance to get set, no chance to light a pipe, no chance to relax. You act like you thought time was money. That's a proverb, isn't it, Rig? 'Time is money'?"

"I don't know," Rig said weakly.

Tip swung his leg down, as if he were going to get up.

Rig started to rise, and Tip settled back in the chair and threw the other leg up.

"A proverb," Tip repeated. "That reminds me, Rig. My old man loved proverbs. He was a great reader." He looked sharply at Rig. "Did you know that?"

"I—didn't know your old man," Rig said hoarsely.

"That's right, you didn't. Well, he liked to read. He was after what he called a philosophy of life, and he figured he'd look for it this way. Are you listenin', Rig?"

"Yes," Rig whispered. His face had gone to pieces now.

"He'd read all the proverbs he could find. But you know, Rig, for some proverbs that sound wise you can find other proverbs that contradict them. Let me see." Tip looked at the ceiling. "Here's two that contradict each other. 'Make haste slowly,' and 'Nothing ventured, nothing gained.' See? They cancel each other, don't they?"

Rig nodded, his eyes desperate.

"Well, my old man got all the proverbs together, threw away all those that canceled out, and guess what he had left? It was his philosophy of life. Do you know what it was?"

"No."

Tip swung his leg over the chair arm and came to his feet. Rig came to his feet, too.

"It was this. 'When you're dead, you're dead!' And Rig, you're dead!"

Rig clawed away from him, and Tip grabbed him by the shirt front. He reached in under his coat and brought out Rig's gun and threw it toward Lynn. Then he shoved Rig into a corner.

"Tip, Tip!" Rig pleaded. "Don't shoot me! I'll split it with you, Tip. No, I'll give it to you if you'll let me go!"

Tip stood there unbuckling his gun belt. He let it drop to the floor, then kicked it over in Lynn's direction.

"Shoot you?" Tip drawled. "Hell, no, Rig. That's too easy a way to die for a maggot like you. I'm goin' to peel the skin off your back and see if it's yellow clear down to the bone."

"Don't, Tip!" Lynn said.

Tip didn't hear her. He swung Rig out of the corner and knocked him over the footboard of the bed. The bed gave in at both ends and crashed to the floor. Rig scrambled up and backed against the wall. Pure terror was on his face.

"Tip, I'll give you all the money I got if you'll let me go!"

"There ain't enough money in the world to buy you off, Rig. Come off that bed!"

Rig Holman saw it was hopeless. He lunged for a chair, and Tip cut across to him and drove a left into his midriff that threw him against the washstand. Rig scrambled to his feet, picked up the water pitcher, and threw it at Tip, who ducked. It crashed into the mirror with a loud jangle and broke against the wall.

Rig had the bowl raised over his head when Tip came at him. He brought it down, and Tip threw up his arm to ward it off. It broke, and a great jagged shard ripped across Tip's cheek, drawing blood; Tip slugged him then, and Rig's head slapped back against the partition and he slid to the floor.

Turning quickly, he kicked up at Tip, catching him on the old wound. Tip's leg crumpled and he went down, and Rig dove on him. The breath slammed out of Tip now, and he felt Rig's slim, strong fingers circle his throat. He wrapped his arms around Rig and squeezed, then kicked with one leg and rolled over. When Rig came under him, he slugged hard at his face, and the thick, slapping sound of knuckle-studded fist on flesh was followed by a moan. Rig turned and sank his teeth into Tip's hand.

Tip came off him, yanking his hand away, and Rig scrambled to his feet now. Lynn, the gun still in her hand, her eyes wide with terror, was backed into a corner. Rig made a dash for the door, and Tip lunged against it. Tip threw him into a corner, then came at him. His back to the wall, Rig Holman had to fight now. He slugged out, and Tip did the same, standing toe to toe with him. Sud-

denly Rig ducked and then kicked out. Tip twisted, and
the kick caught him in the side and he went down across
the doorway. Rig leaped across the room, threw open the
window, and put a leg out. Then he looked down and
drew back, just as Tip reached him. Rig turned now, fury
and terror and stark panic in his eyes. He fought like a
wildcat, scratching and kicking and cursing through
bloody lips. His coat was ripped off his back, and he was
dragging it by one sleeve.

Tip's shirt was in tatters, and his face streaked with
blood. But now he was fighting coolly, viciously, watching
Rig's legs, watching for his openings. Time after time he
smashed in blows at Rig's face, and each time Rig tried to
dodge away from the open window, Tip stopped him with
a rocketing blow that sent him back against the sill.

Lynn was crying, "Oh, Tip, don't. Let him go!" And
Tip didn't hear her. Suddenly, Rig lunged at Tip, his
arms wide to grab him and hold on to him. Tip caught
his lunge, feet planted, and heaved forward. The sill
caught Rig in the back and he bent outside. His scream
for help keened into the night.

Holding him that way, with his right hand around
Rig's throat, Tip slugged him in the face with all his
strength and all his weight. He hit him so hard that he
tore his own grip loose, and Rig went farther back still,
taking Tip, who was off balance, too, with him. Tip
grabbed for the window and got it and saw Rig's body
slide over the sill, clear it, turn once in the air, and then
hit the ground two stories below.

He pulled himself back into the room, and then looked
at Lynn. Her face was drained of color and she was looking at Tip with eyes that were dark with fright.

"Oh, Tip," she moaned, "don't look that way."

"Give me that gun," Tip said, and walked across the
room, his hand outstretched. Lynn gave it to him, and Tip
took it in his hand and opened the door and went out.
He went downstairs, Lynn behind him, and through the
lobby and out to the corner and rounded it.

There were many people already around Rig Holman, and Tip shoved them out of his way until he was standing beside Rig. Joerns, next to the man holding the lantern, stepped aside, and Tip kneeled by Rig and rolled him over.

Rig Holman was dead, his neck broken. Tip let him roll back on his face, feeling all the strength and rage drain out of him.

He looked up at Lynn, who eyed him silently, and then at Joerns. He stood up, swaying slightly.

"There's the man who killed Blackie Mayfell," Tip said to Joerns.

"All right," Joerns said.

Tip thought of something then. He reached down to the tattered rag of a coat that trailed out behind Rig and felt in the coat pocket. He drew out a paper, opened it, and then rose and walked over to Joerns.

"This is the deed you gave Rig Holman, isn't it, Joerns?"

"Why—yes."

Tip ripped it in half, in quarters, in eighths, then threw the pieces in Joerns's face. The banker backed up, and Tip grabbed his coat and hauled him to him.

"Joerns, I'm still deputy sheriff of Vermilion county and Ball is sheriff. I'll dare you to tell any man, here and now, that Rig Holman owns that ranch."

Joerns tried to pull away and couldn't, and his face went slack with fear.

"Then—who does own it?"

"Buck Shields owns it!" Tip ripped out. "He's comin' back here and run it, too. You better tell this crowd that any bounty money your bank has put up is withdrawn, too. Tell 'em now!"

Joerns said weakly, "I withdraw it!"

Tip let go of him and pushed him back into the silent spectators, then looked over the crowd. "There's a lot of things you people have been wrong-guessin' on besides me," he said. "None of it matters much, I reckon, but that Buck Shields and Anna Bolling are gettin' married. This

Vermilion county feud is over, for plumb good and all. Buck Shields has found gold under that place of his. If he wants to, he can hire a hundred gunmen to come in this town and pull it down on your heads. It's up to you people. Are you goin' to fight, or are you goin' to let the only straight Bolling and the Shieldses come back here and live in peace, like they want to?"

"Gold!" Joerns said. "Is that what Holman was after?"

"He was after it and he didn't get it!" Tip said belligerently. He looked over the crowd. "Well, what'll it be?"

Someone back in the crowd drawled, "Hell, Red, you can't lick us all. Sure we'll give Buck Shields a chance, and Anna Bolling, too. They don't fight, we don't fight. Is that right?"

A murmur of assent rose from the crowd. Tip said, "There's one way a dozen of you men can prove that."

"How?"

"Go up there and pull Pate Shields out of jail and give him a horse and send the kid home."

There was a moment of silence, and then someone yelled, "Come on."

Tip grinned then, and the tension was gone. He found Lynn by his side and he went into the hotel with her. They didn't talk; there was nothing to say now in this moment.

"Come up and let me wash your cuts," Lynn said, her voice businesslike and flat.

They went up to her room, and while Tip stood there in the middle of the floor, his shirt trailing down behind him, Lynn washed the blood off his face and arms. Tip watched her deft work, felt her light touch as she worked.

"So it was Rig who shot at me when I went into the sheriff's office?" he asked finally.

"I think so," Lynn said, pausing in her work. "He came up the stairs carrying a rifle. I was watching his room. When he went in, I slipped into Uncle Dave's room and told him. He got up to help me."

"Thanks for keepin' him for me."

"Let's don't talk about it, Tip," Lynn said quietly.

"I told you it wouldn't be pretty. I reckon I lost my temper."

Lynn looked up at him and smiled faintly. "Your temper, Tip. Think what it's done for you. It brought you to this town. It got you into this feud. It got you into so many fights that the town rose in disgust to drive you out. It's got you into nothing but trouble."

Tip scratched his head. "That's right," he said quietly. He looked obliquely at her. "Still, it helped to win this fight, sort of."

Lynn paused in her work, staring at him. "Tip, you aren't apologizing for it, are you?"

"Well—sort of."

"But why?"

Tip looked at her closely, and the color crept into his face. "This is goin' to be hard to say, Lynn."

"Then get mad at it."

Tip didn't laugh then. "Out there at the camp on the line, you told me that night that you almost believed my roughneck way was the only way to settle this fight, didn't you?"

"Yes, I did."

"Well," Tip said, fumbling for the right words, "all I got in my life has been with those roughneck ways, with fightin'. And to fight I got to get mad. And to get mad, I got to lose my temper."

"Well?" Lynn said, looking at him.

"A minute ago you were combin' me over for losin' my temper, sayin' it had got me into all my trouble. But I've got to fight to get anything." He paused. "You don't believe I ought to, do you?"

Lynn looked at him impatiently. "Tip, I'm going to go back to that same night at the camp. Do you remember you said that you were in this fight to earn money? You said you felt ashamed of yourself. Remember?"

"Sure."

"Do you realize that you haven't got your money, that you never will, that Rig Holman is dead? Do you realize

that you came up here, talked to him, fo
and beat him, and not once did you think of what y
would get out of it?"

"I—I lost my temper."

Lynn laughed. "That's it, Tip." When Tip tried to
speak, Lynn held up her hand. "Let me say it for you, Tip.
You're wondering if I could ever love a man with red hair,
a man who loses his temper often, but always at the right
time. You're wondering if you could ask me to marry you.
Is that it?"

Tip nodded mutely.

"My answer is pretty simple, Tip. I'll say yes now, if
you can find words to ask me."

Tip put his hands on her arms. "Lynn, will you take a
chance and marry me?"

Lynn laughed with delight and said, "Of course, Tip.
It's not even a chance." And Tip folded her to him and
held her close, feeling her warm body against his, knowing
that something was worth fighting for and that he was
holding it in his arms.